THE ACCIDENTAL
AGENT

Madhav Gokhlay

Order this book online at www.trafford.com
or email orders@trafford.com

Most Trafford titles are also available at major online book retailers.

Printed in the United States of America.

ISBN: 978-1-4669-2928-9 (sc)
ISBN: 978-1-4669-2927-2 (hc)
ISBN: 978-1-4669-2926-5 (e)

Library of Congress Control Number: 2012906935

Trafford rev. 05/01/2012

 www.trafford.com

North America & international
toll-free: 1 888 232 4444 (USA & Canada)
phone: 250 383 6864 ✦ fax: 812 355 4082

In Memory of
My mother who always inspired me
Even in her last days

ACKNOWLEDGEMENTS

This book would not have been possible without help and support from my family and friends. Special thanks to my wife and children for guiding the story line and editing the book.

CHAPTER 1

With a thundering roar of its engines, all one hundred and fifty tons of the Airbus A300 lifted up into the air. The skies above Newark Liberty International airport were busy as usual. Inside, passengers seated in various degrees of comfort felt a sense of relief that the flight was finally on its way. They had waited patiently while the plane taxied away from the gate and then just waited on the runway for more than an hour due to traffic congestion.

Sid folded the airline magazine he was browsing and pushed it in the seat pocket in front of him. He had looked it over from cover to cover and had attempted the crossword puzzle. His mind was tired. The hectic schedule of the last several days had taken its toll. The flight already seemed quite boring. *Seventeen more hours of this?* he complained to himself. He was on his second overseas trip in this job and his first real assignment. The last trip was part of his training. *Or was it just training?* He wondered. He wasn't sure he had understood ways of the CIA.

"So, what's your trip for? Business? Or pleasure?" The words floated to his groggy brain. Sid fought through the layers of lethargy that had engulfed his tired mind. His neighbor for the next seventeen hours was starting a polite conversation. Sid looked to his right again, this time paying attention to who was sitting there.

"Oh, it's certainly not for pleasure." He said, addressing the gentleman sitting in the window seat. The plane had two aisles, which made for three columns of seats in the coach class. Each row was laid out with a cluster of three seats at both flanks and five seats in the middle. Sid had an aisle seat on the starboard side. Thankfully, the seat between him and his neighbor was not occupied, which gave them both some extra knee and elbow room.

"I'm going for work. What about you?"

"I'm joining my wife in Goa." replied the gentleman with a bubbly eagerness unique to the infrequent traveler. He was obviously a tourist.

"That's nice; I've heard it's a great place to visit to get some sun." Sid politely continued the small talk for a few more minutes.

Soon the airplane reached a high-enough altitude and the usual robotic voice announced that passengers could now use their electronic devices. Sid reclined his seat, put on the noise cancelling headphones he had received as a gift from his parents. It was his graduation gift, a practical gift as usual. He had a job offer before graduation and his parents knew he was supposed to leave for an assignment in Europe. Well, he was getting good use out of the gift. Sid had tucked away eye shade in his pocket. He took them out and snapped them on his eyes. He needed some sleep.

But despite his deliberate preparation, sleep eluded him. Sid could never sleep on airplanes. His mind was going over last one year of his life, graduating from college and accepting this job with the CIA. His current mission, if he could call it a mission, didn't seem like what CIA field agents would normally do. But then he thought of Poland and Hungary. His training stints there didn't feel like CIA assignments either, until the last two months. He remembered the exciting tasks of secretive drops and pickups of various information assets, ranging from bulky envelopes to computer chips. Unfortunately, he had no idea which or how many of those tasks were simple exercises as part of his training, and which were for the real CIA business.

He had joined the CIA in July of last year. After three months at the Langley campus and almost seven months of work in Europe, mostly in Eastern Europe, he was recalled prematurely from his field training. Sid was surprised because his handler and mentor at the CIA had arranged a one day visit to meet with his professor at

Cromwell University. Professor Levine had talked to Sid at length about his next assignment. It was an awkward conversation with a man he had known so well. Sid was taken aback by the fact that it was his professor who briefed him and not someone in the CIA. As far as Sid knew, Professor Levine didn't play any active role outside of academia. Sid of course knew that the Professor had a good friend somewhere high up in government. In fact that's how he had got a job offer with the CIA. *But active involvement?*

Sid had hoped to meet Sarah while he was being briefed by Professor Levine, but she was not on campus. She was visiting her mother in Kansas. He wished he had an advanced notice of his trip to the campus, so he could have planned to meet her. There was so much that he had bottled up inside him over the past year. But he couldn't wait around for her on campus. He was flying out to Birmingham immediately after his meeting with Professor Levine, to see his parents and to get the official CIA briefing of this assignment. Sid was grateful that he didn't have to go to Langley. It was nice to see his parents after a long stay overseas. As much as he didn't want to admit, going home always helped him adjust his internal compass and reaffirm the solid grounding in values he grew up with.

"Anything to drink?" A flight attendant queried. Sid pulled off his eye shades and flashed a smile.

"A coke please. Coke Zero if you have it."

"Certainly." The flight attendant gave him a can of Coke Zero and a cup filled with ice. Then she put down several packets of peanuts and cookies. After all, Sid had a charming smile.

Sid decided to give up his attempt to sleep and focus on the current assignment. He was feeling uneasy after the talk with Professor Levine, but surprisingly, his official briefing from Brad Malone was as if Sid was going on a trip for pleasure. Except at the very end, Brad had asked him what exactly he was going to do in Pune India.

"Don't you know?" Sid asked, totally surprised by Brad's question.

He then quickly covered what Professor Levine had told him, instinctively omitting some detail as he went along. His encounter with the CIA, right from day one, was not very comfortable. He remembered his first several weeks on the job, filled with indoctrinations and briefings from various characters that came and went like specialists in a hospital, talking at a patient rather than to a patient. Sid was relieved that the same story was not repeated this time around. His job over the next several months was to blend in and be known in India's high tech circles. That's all he shared with Brad, anyways. He didn't feel like sharing the uncomfortable part of his conversation with Professor Levine. If Brad didn't know about it then perhaps it was meant to be that way. He was already behaving like an experienced agent.

The flight was uneventful and boringly long. Sid even looked to his neighbor for some more small talk. But his neighbor was fast asleep. *Lucky man,* Sid muttered under his breath.

The flight landed at Mumbai's *Chatrapati Shivaj* International Airport. Sid went through the Immigration check, collected his bags and exited the airport. Hot, humid air slapped Sid in the face. Summer in Mumbai India can be very uncomfortable with the hot, still air that never cools down enough to let one breathe easily. Sid knew from his briefing that the monsoon rains would bring some relief, but that was at least a few weeks away.

Outside the airport a dark complexioned, rather tall man with thick black moustache was standing with a placard raised high above his head, towering over a throng of drivers, taxi brokers and eager relatives of non-resident Indians returning to their homeland for a visit. The sign read, 'Sid Joshi, CryptoTech Pvt Ltd'. That's exactly what Brad had told him to expect. Sid wasn't convinced it was a real company. He remembered his days in Eastern Europe and realized he was already missing the excitement of the 'cloak and dagger' part of the training. But he had not signed up for such thrills. This job was strictly a white collar job, that of a computer security specialist, as he was told during the recruitment process. And of course his professor, Dr. Levine had approached him with similar understanding.

The words of his CIA trainer and mentor Brad Malone were fresh in Sid's mind.

"Remember one thing Sid. Not everyone on the CIA payroll carries a gun or even knows how to use one."

Brad was a mid-rank career officer in CIA and worked in the cyber-crime division. Brad was tall and muscular at hundred and sixty pounds. He had worked as a field agent for ten years before quitting the CIA to pursue a Masters degree in Computer Information Systems, an unlikely choice for a CIA field agent. After graduation, it was an easy decision to rejoin the agency. The CIA had been paying more attention to computer technology than ever before, and Brad's profile fit the CIA requirements like hand in a glove. After spending three years in the new job, Brad's distinguished record had convinced the CIA deputy director to focus on recruiting multi-disciplinary talent and Brad was put in the newly created position. Brad Malone's job was to bring on board young recruits and guide them through their first year on the job. The one year program was designed by Brad to provide the recruits with a real feel for how most of the human intelligence was gathered, filtered and relayed to analysts. Brad recommended and the deputy director agreed, that analysts would be able to conduct a far better analysis of information they get if they knew how the information was gathered. This was deemed necessary so the analysts could effectively tune the computer-aided, artificial intelligence programs that were constantly being developed to give better results.

To his recruits, Brad Malone was a friend, a mentor and a disciplinarian, all rolled into one.

"The best job a field agent can do is to gather cold, hard facts on the ground and turn them into useful information for someone to evaluate and act on." Brad used to say.

"A good field agent mixes well into his or her surroundings. During your training, I want you to think and act like people around you in the field. Because when you are at the other end of this information flow, getting input from the field, I want you to have a real sense of how these people operate and what methods they use to gather the information. You will have to sift through what you get and make a call on how to interpret the information."

These words were echoing in Sid's ears as he approached the driver holding the sign.

"I am Sid Joshi." he said extending his hand.

"I am Anand, Sir. Welcome to India Sir." The driver introduced himself. Sid felt a little uncomfortable being addressed as Sir. Anand took charge of Sid's bags as they walked a short distance to a SUV in the parking deck. Anand whisked the car out of the congested parking area and onto the dark streets of Mumbai. It was past midnight.

Sid was grateful for the whisperingly quiet air conditioning. They travelled for an hour or maybe longer before the car weaved its way through the winding stretch of the road called the *Western Ghat,* between Mumbai and Pune, climbing some 1800 feet to reach India's Deccan Plateau.

Sid's apartment was small but comfortable. Situated in an area called Kothrud, a middle-class enclave in Pune, it was well furnished, air-conditioned and most importantly its pantry was stocked with Sid's personal favorite food items.

"Don't eat outside except for these restaurants." Brad had told him handing him a list of names and locations on a detailed map of Pune.

That's just great, thought Sid sarcastically. *This is exactly what I dreamt of on my first India visit as an adult.*

Sid had made a few trips to India as a child travelling with his parents. But this was different. This was part of his job. Sid wasn't quite sure yet that this job was the right one for him. He often thought about his days as a fresh CIA recruit going through the orientation. On this first assignment past the field training, Sid was already rethinking the wisdom of accepting this job. But in the end Sid had made a commitment and he wasn't afraid of commitments once he made them. Perseverance was one of his qualities that had served him well.

He reached in his pocket and retrieved a mobile phone that his driver Anand had given him. He dialed Brad's number to report his safe arrival in the apartment, although Sid was dead sure that through the CIA channels Brad already knew the relevant facts.

CHAPTER 2

General Iqbal Chaudhry was an imposing figure. He was well built and stood strong and erect, like a teak tree. Even at his age of late sixties, he exuded raw physical power. He looked, talked and acted every bit like the army man he was. His thick moustache had turned a mixture of salt and pepper. In his olive green military uniform, donning a felt cap slanted to the left, and wearing expensive sun glasses, he was an embodiment of authority and power.

General Chaudhry was elite in Pakistan's army, and he had served his country honorably. Pakistan was the country his father called his own, and where Iqbal was raised since the age of five. He was of tender age when the partition of British India took place. What started out as an exercise of the political will of one man, soon exploded into an unparalleled mass migration in the Indian sub-continent. And making things worse, what started as an orderly and willing migration of people to their promised land, took an ugly and bloody turn. It was that historic event that had brought Iqbal Chaudhry's family to Pakistan. When the waves of the bloody migration subsided, Iqbal's father and his family found themselves swept up somewhere in the Punjab province that became part of Pakistan.

Almost all of his family had made it to their new country. During the chaotic days of the partition, families were separated; people on both sides, Hindus and Muslims, were slaughtered. By one account the death toll reached almost a million, although no one knows for sure. More than ten million people were displaced, travelling to their respective new country by whatever means they could muster. Trains filled with people left both sides of the new border in anxious anticipation, but they didn't reach their destinations in peace. Mass graves and mass cremation became the norm as those left alive couldn't deal with the number of dead bodies. It was a nightmare that gave birth to two nations. But unlike the birthing pains that soon go away with a loving touch of the newborn, General Chaudhry's father bore scars of that era to his grave. Little Iqbal grew up with bitterness stemming from the partition. The bitterness had developed in a grudge he harbored as a child and had eventually progressed into full scale hatred as an adult.

His older sister Hina, who was eight years old at the time, was one of the missing people in the upheaval of the partition. Iqbal's father never forgave himself for letting it happen. For many years his father hoped that his daughter was alive somewhere and would reunite with her family. There wasn't a day when his father didn't think of his daughter. And the family, including little Iqbal, always kept her memory alive. The wound left by that horrific loss had never healed. His father's perpetual grievance had made a deep emotional chasm in young Iqbal.

Bloody Hindus, Iqbal would spit out, like a snake striking its venom.

The general turned away from old memories with great effort. He was an army man. Having risen through the ranks, now a general no less, Iqbal Chaudhry was a proud and fiercely patriotic man. He was a son of a *muhajir* and as such, a healthy portion of that patriotism was of course loathing for India. But what ate him was more than rage. He was also envious of that ever prospering so called secular nation.

But blind hatred had no place in his world. That was the forte of the *mujahedeen* fools who were ready to blow themselves up at the slightest encouragement. Hatred had to be translated into an action to hurt the enemy where it really counted, and not merely kill a few people. The three wars with India since the partition were just skirmishes. A real lesson would be taught soon, he thought to himself.

"I beg your pardon Sir." A polite voice jolted general Chaudhry back to reality.

"You have a call from the Yankees, sir. *Kuch khaas baat hai.*"

Iqbal Chaudhry ran a tight ship, by the book. His orderly was prohibited to use *Urdu*, but every now and then he slipped. Yusuf Gilani, his orderly, was a loyal assistant of over twenty five years. Through his meteoric rise in the army, Iqbal Chaudhry had helped many people. During the 1971 War with India, Iqbal Chaudhry was a colonel. His unit had fought valiantly at the ground war in Punjab. He had saved the life of one Yusuf Gilani during the assault by the Indian army. Although he lost the battle, General Chaudhry had made many lifelong friends. And in the case of Yusuf Gilani, he had gained loyalty of a grateful foot soldier who had vowed to serve him for the rest of his life.

Yusuf Gilani's use of *Urdu* was a minor irritant in the bigger picture. And General Chaudhry was all about the big picture. He held the strategic post of a special advisor to the chief of the ISI, Pakistan's elite secret service agency. It was rumored both inside and outside Pakistan that the ISI, Inter Services Intelligence agency was the real king maker in Pakistan. One of the few institutions that worked well in Pakistan was its army and ISI was the army's crown jewel.

Sadly, the army and especially the ISI, was much maligned lately. Ever since the U.S. raid that killed Osama bin Laden in *Abbotabad*, the army had lost respect domestically. He would never forgive the Americans for that. Unfortunately, he still needed the American aid which had dried up in the last few months.

"I'll take the call in my office." said the general as he took powerful strides through the plush hallway of his Karachi residence, towards his office equipped with the latest communication gear.

CHAPTER 3

Roger Patel eased his bright yellow Lamborghini Diablo into the now thinning traffic on California's highway 101, the artery of the Silicon Valley. Roger was used to envious stares from fellow riders on the road; after all, this car was his trophy, symbolizing everything he had achieved and who he was.

Roger tapped his fingers on the luxurious steering wheel and glided into the leftmost lane as the comforting hum of the car's five hundred and thirty horses took over his troubled mind. He secretly knew that the car was his best therapy to cope with the enormous pressures of his business. Roger was self driven to a fault. As if running a large business wasn't enough, he incessantly tried to outsmart and outmaneuver his peers to establish his personal superiority. Lately he was finding it hard to keep up with his own burning ambition.

Born in a rich family in Bombay, now called Mumbai, his original name was Rajan Patel. Rajan grew up in the exclusive neighborhood of Pedar Road in South Mumbai. He enjoyed every possible creature comfort throughout his childhood. Rajan's father was an influential real estate developer in Mumbai. It was said that the senior Patel controlled or had influence over almost one third of the real estate market in South Mumbai, which was an exclusive area in Bombay ever since the time of British occupation. As the city developed, there was more demand for land. Mumbai is a peninsula, surrounded by sea on three sides except the North. An insatiable demand for office and high end residential buildings had resulted in man's triumph over nature by reclaiming land from the sea. Rajan's father was instrumental in making it happen and naturally he also had a lion's share of this new expensive property.

But no amount of reclamation was enough and the city was growing vertically, putting up skyscrapers at an alarming speed. There was a period in the 1980s when real estate in South Mumbai was among the most expensive in the world, even eclipsing Tokyo's real estate market for a few short months.

Rajan was a precocious child. He showed very early signs of both raw intelligence and a fiercely competitive spirit. His father recognized his son's talents. He groomed and encouraged Rajan to be a go-getter. Rajan was enrolled in prestigious private schools and was tutored by the finest in teaching profession. Rajan easily catapulted through the schools and got himself into one of the famed Indian Institute of Technology engineering universities. These schools, known in India as IITs, were fiercely competitive to get admission into. Unlike many other institutions in India at that time, money or influence couldn't affect the schools' decision to admit students. Rajan, a bright young man of seventeen had enrolled into the double-E or the Electrical and Electronic engineering curriculum, one of the most sought after branches of engineering at that time.

In addition to the high quality of education, these institutions also required that students live on campus unlike many other colleges. As part of the tough curriculum, Rajan had left home to live in a dormitory room on campus which was located in the northern part of the city. His years away from home had given Rajan a chance to grow personally and create his own identity. It changed Rajan from a brash, rich kid to a mature, ambitious and a driven young man. During his years at the college, Rajan was morphed into Roger as the Western, especially American, influence won him over. He preferred to be called by his new name and his friends obliged. From then on he was known to all as Roger.

The core engineering curriculum was augmented by requiring students to take one non-engineering course every semester. Economics was one of the required courses in his curriculum, which

Roger developed a great liking for. He eagerly absorbed the entire textbook authored by a famous American economist. He was thrilled to talk about free markets, spirit of entrepreneurship and supply and demand setting prices for goods and services. He didn't know back then that the very ideas storming through his young mind in college and the free spirit of America were going to make him rich beyond his imagination. And perhaps it was also something that would ultimately push him over the edge.

Roger shifted down and changed lanes to take an exit. Ever since his strange meeting with Jim Arnold, Roger had felt uneasiness in his chest. He had often experienced similar feeling before closing big business deals. But there was something different this time, and he couldn't quite put a finger on it although he knew deep inside that he was perhaps playing with the Devil himself.

CHAPTER 4

"**S**iddarth *beta*, come down for breakfast." called out Mrs. Savita Joshi hoping to get through the loud music emanating from Siddarth's room upstairs.

"You have to get ready to leave for college in one hour."

It was a beautiful spring morning in March. Hedgerows of Forsythia were bright yellow with new growth. Azaleas were about to burst into hundreds of bright flowers. Chirruping cardinals, robins and other non-descript birds fluttered around in the backyard, trying to get the bird feed that escaped squirrel raids. Fescue grass in the backyard was showing healthy dark green growth although Bermuda grass in the front yard took until summer before turning green.

The house was situated in suburban Birmingham, Alabama where Mrs. Joshi, Siddarth's mother, was cajoling her favorite son, her only son, to be on time.

"*Itna bada ho gaya lekin ab tak time ka hosh nahin aaya.*" she complained halfheartedly, under her breath. Like many mothers, she was complaining about the lack of time management on part of her son. But her husband heard her.

Mr. Vasant Joshi, Siddarth's father, glanced up from the weekend edition of Wall Street Journal he was reading and shook his head.

"Let him be, why are you always on his case? He is old enough to manage all by himself."

The Joshi household was a typical professional middle class immigrant family from India. Mr. and Mrs. Joshi were part of what was once termed as 'brain drain' in India. In nineteen seventies and eighties, there was a passionate debate in India about so many well educated young adults leaving the country to go abroad, especially to the United States of America. The argument was that loss of these young, talented resources would surely hurt the motherland. The counter argument was that the education system was perhaps preparing these science and engineering graduates ahead of the industry demand for them. So what were they supposed to do if they couldn't find the right job in India?

However, after twenty five years or so, intellectuals both in India and in the U.S. based Indian community realized that the 'brain drain' argument didn't hold water in this highly global and competitive economy. Over the long haul, emigration of the few educated citizens was not necessarily a loss for India. In fact, it was proving to be a net positive as the Indian economy became more open to the outside world. These early emigrants had proven themselves in their new country to be talented, diligent workers. A crop of entrepreneurs from that population had started businesses which tapped tremendous and readily available talent back home, thus creating an entire new segment of Information Technology outsourcing business in India.

The story of immigrants making a success for themselves was by no means unique in America, the land of immigrants. Mr. Joshi and his wife, whom he had met in college, were similar to thousands of others, who had worked hard, played by the rules and had achieved good bit of success, a manifestation of the American dream. Lately though, the dark clouds of outsourcing high-tech jobs were gathering on Mr. Joshi's horizon. The newspaper he was reading, constantly reminded him of the job losses taking place by the thousands, but its editorial pages were full of praise of the free enterprise and extolled virtues of laissez-faire approach by the previous administration. And the current administration was so bogged down by serious economic problems that it couldn't and didn't do anything about the job loss problem.

Mr. Joshi heard thuds of footsteps coming from the stairs and put down his newspaper.

Siddarth Joshi, called Sid by his friends, was a senior at Cromwell University. About to graduate at the top of his class, the handsome young man was in his prime. At five feet eleven, tall by his family standard, Sid was athletic, built from six straight years of lacrosse. He had joined the high school lacrosse team in his sophomore year out of boredom. The high school coach very quickly realized that this boy had superb acumen for the game, so he worked on Sid to get him physically fit as a starter for the Junior Varsity team and the very next year Sid easily made into the Varsity team. His mother of course worried about sport injuries but soon resigned to the fact that no matter what she thought, her little boy was little no more and could take and give blows with ease.

Sid was drying up his hair with a towel as he came down the stairs. *Can't be late for breakfast,* he thought to himself. His mom was making chocolate pancakes he loved as a child. He didn't care much for them anymore, but just couldn't bring himself to come out and say it aloud. Besides, a little chocolate from time to time was not too bad.

He had another reason to hurry. Sid was going to drop off his Ducati motorcycle at a dealer to sell it. Sid had bought a used Ducati in his college sophomore year against his parents' wishes. He had saved money from various campus jobs and gifts from relatives. He couldn't take the motorcycle all the way to Ithaca, so he used to ride and repair it at home during college breaks. Ithaca was too cold to ride a motorcycle anyways. Sid had decided to sell the motorcycle and was hoping to break even as he had put in a lot of work improving the motorcycle from the time he bought it from a neighbor.

Sid was about to return back to Cromwell after the last break of his undergraduate years. There was a potential job offer he was thinking about. Professor Levine had spoken to him about this opportunity in private. The job was not listed in the placement office, which was unusual. Besides, the edge in Dr. Levine's voice had left Sid somewhat puzzled. *But there will be time for all that later,* he thought to himself.

CHAPTER 5

As far as lobbyists in Washington D.C. go, they come in all sizes of their influence and depth or lack thereof, of their moral character. Jim Arnold firmly believed that morality had nothing to do with his job. He would leave that to the men of collar. He had a business to run. Money was the ultimate God and his ability to influence others was the trading tool that made him money, lots of money.

Arnold & Gregg was a very successful lobbying firm in Washington D.C. Situated to the east of Potomac, among the throng of offices on the K Street, their office building was not a run of the mill generic structure. Standing twelve stories high with an old style architecture façade, the building clearly demonstrated the class and aplomb, so essential to doing business in this city. The firm owned and occupied the entire building. Arnold & Gregg had their fingers in almost everything commercially important that happened in Washington D.C. and indeed throughout much of the Western world, wherever tentacles of American influence reached.

The lobby of the building looked more like an art museum than an office building. Two stories high, the lobby displayed numerous original paintings and collectibles that would make many museums envious. Jim Arnold, the owner partner, was known to give a tour of the lobby to his distinguished guests. And there were always many important clients, some of them perhaps not distinguished in a social sense, but important nonetheless, that walked the lobby. The building had an army of security guards and modern surveillance equipment befitting a diplomatic mission.

Arnold & Gregg had clients from all walks of life. Not unlike a Swiss bank, protecting privacy of its clients was of paramount importance. In fact the firm had an elaborate policy and a set of procedures to accomplish just that. Every potential client wishing to stay out of the public eye would get a briefing from the firm's senior management on the steps the firm would take to protect the client's anonymity. The building even had a couple of lesser known entrances from the alleyway to the backside. These access points were known to be used by some nefarious third world strongmen on insistence from the firm.

Jim Arnold wielded enormous influence in this politically charged town. He had a huge chest of political favors that others owed him, and he would cash in every one of them in due course. Jim had methodically collected these political IOUs from the now influential politicians and bureaucrats. His methods were not always beyond reproach, but then Jim had very non-traditional views on morality. It was something for the men of collar, not him.

As usual Jim was multi-tasking at his party tonight. One of his objectives was to cast a net for catching another IOU in his stockpile. Jim was always on the lookout for the well connected Washington insiders to beef up his employee base. He had found and recruited Todd Lester about six months earlier. But Todd wasn't malleable enough to fit in Jim's mold just yet. *Need to get this guy a little relaxed and to open up,* Jim thought.

Todd Lester was a devout Christian. He would never miss a Sunday service, and always donated generously to his Arlington church. A big man, at 240 pounds, Todd was a career Pentagon bureaucrat. A graduate of the college of William & Mary, he had started work in the Pentagon at an early age during the Carter administration. Young Todd, an apolitical figure at that time, had witnessed the Iran hostage fiasco and he squarely put the blame on President Jimmy Carter. From then on his political views were shaped by the rise of the conservative movement in America. Being hard working and moderately talented has its merits in government service. Longevity was the name of the game. Todd was steadily promoted and had developed reputation as a straight arrow. Superiors counted on his unbiased approach which he meticulously maintained despite his changing political views. Defense contractors knew him as neither an ally nor a foe, so they generally left him alone.

Todd and his wife Jill couldn't have children of their own. Todd was very close to his nephew Michael, his sister's son. One can say he had sort of adopted this nephew, caring for him deeply. Todd was the one to insist that Michael should go to a private college, which Michael did, thanks to financial help from Uncle Todd.

During the George W. Bush years, Todd had become an assistant secretary in the Pentagon's massive bureaucracy, a significant achievement. As he got older however, Todd grew more and more dissatisfied with the nation's steady decline, both in terms of its moral character and the loss of its manufacturing, and more recently its high value white collar jobs to competition overseas. Having seen the culture of corruption in the Pentagon, there came a point when Todd thought, *what the heck, if you can't beat them, then join them.* With his myriad connections in Pentagon, it was an easy thing to find a job at the prestigious lobbying firm of Arnold and Gregg. The job paid well, far better than he could have ever hoped for in the government service. Todd knew that his newly found road to riches was paved with certain expectations. His boss, Jim Arnold had not yet demanded a pound of flesh, but Todd knew that day was coming. It was his hope to delay the inevitable for as long as he could.

The party atmosphere at the Blue Pearl was intoxicating. A prestigious nightclub on the 14th street, the place was frequented by the rich and powerful seeking some fun out of the public eye. Although not very glitzy from the outside, the club had a Las Vegas style interior with several dance floors catering to different tastes in music. There were huge, inviting bars stocked with every imaginable drink and staffed by the best in bartending profession. The bar tenders were picked after exhaustive vetting process and were known to be dependable. And they were rewarded for their discretion. There were several niches where comfortable sofas and chairs were arranged just at a right distance from the dance floor music so a confidential conversation could take place without being overheard.

Arnold and Gregg had rented the entire club for one of their bashes. The list of invitees obviously included both current and potential clients as well as those who either owed favors to the firm or were being sought after by the firm for their political or social influence. As a senior member of the firm, Todd was invited to these parties since joining the firm, but he had found some excuse to not attend. But not tonight.

Jill was out of town and Todd had decided to go by himself. He needed to get out some more, he thought.

"There you are, my man." thundered Jim Arnold, the veritable marketing man and a major influence peddler in Washington circles.

"Glad to see you are here Todd. Enjoy yourself and then I want you to meet someone."

Todd flashed a broad smile and shook hands with his gracious host and boss. He was somewhat out of his elements in a surrounding like this, but he knew it was part of the job to be there. Todd heaved a sigh of resignation and walked to a passing server carrying champagne glasses. He picked up a glass, closed his eyes for a moment and took a large sip of the Champagne.

He was about to saunter towards the hors d'oeuvres table when he noticed a beautiful young lady at the end of the table eyeing him with some interest. She must be in her early thirties, with a body that could easily turn heads. Todd had always been faithful to his wife, but lately their marriage had been under stress, not unlike many other couples married that long. However, not having the common bond of children coupled with the long hours Todd was known to work had made it harder to deal with the marital strife. In fact he had had a fight with Jill that morning. Many untrue and unfortunate words were thrown around by both spouses and that's why Jill had stormed out of the house, ostensibly to see a relative out of town.

Todd looked at the siren from the corner of his eye. She was now approaching him with a seductive gait and a smile that could just melt a man.

Oh Boy. He whispered under his breath.

CHAPTER 6

The natural beauty of upstate New York is breathtaking. Nestled in verdant landscape near the picturesque Finger Lakes, Ithaca can easily be mistaken as no more than rustic, rural America. But then there is the Cromwell University; alma mater of many a great scholars and scientists. The university is situated on a hill overlooking Ithaca. What brought Professor Dr. Richard Levine to Ithaca was not this natural beauty, but it was surely one of the reasons that made him stay.

Richard J. Levine was an exceptionally brilliant mathematician. After completing graduate studies from Princeton, he resisted the temptation to follow the path of pure mathematics. Unlike mathematicians who stay in pure research, Richard had a natural urge to be innovative in the real, physical world. He found an inviting community in investment banking and in his early career he was instrumental in inventing many complex algorithms for the stock market and investment banking related applications. The systems he helped develop were very profitably implemented by a few key institutions on the Wall Street.

However, in spite of all the money he could make there, Richard soon grew tired of the investment banking field. He needed something new and challenging to keep him going. And that's when he entered the world of cryptography. With his abilities, Richard soon became a well established name in computer cryptology and security. In a short time he amassed many patents in his name. During that time he decided to pursue a Doctoral program at Caltech and decided academia was his calling. After a few years of teaching on the West coast, Dr. Richard Levine accepted a full professorship at the Cromwell University.

During his stay at Caltech, Richard had met a remarkable man from the National Security Agency or NSA, at one of the conferences. After Richard's presentation, Mitch Shelby had approached him and in a few minutes Richard had established a rapport with him. They kept in touch professionally over the years and ended up forming an enduring friendship. Mitch possessed a curious combination of intellect, passion for public policy and an incessant drive to set and reach new goals. He had found an answer to his calling in the U.S. government service where people of Mitch Shelby's qualities were eagerly sought after and nurtured. Mitch had moved among various secret government agencies, but the two men had kept in touch and continued their personal friendship.

The two had formed sort of a ritual. Once a year, they enjoyed summer retreat at the Hilton Head Island with their families. Although Mitch did a lot of highly classified computer security related work, they never really discussed much about his work except making occasional jokes about it. But Richard obviously knew that after 9/11 the world had changed and so had America's security needs and therefore the scope of her spying agencies. His friend, Mitch Shelby, had changed jobs and had assumed added responsibilities, which explained why he had not returned Richard's last two calls. Richard had come up with a ground breaking heuristic algorithm that could shave off significant run time from an artificial intelligence program he had helped develop for the U.S. government. He naturally wanted to run it by his friend to decide whether to publish the findings in a scientific journal or not.

The phone rang and Dr. Richard Levine picked up the receiver.

"Hello" he said.

"Richard, I was in the area and would like to drop by if it's ok."

The familiar voice of Mitch Shelby was on the line.

Richard was surprised. Upstate New York was hardly an area frequented by the Washington types.

"Of course, Mitch." replied Richard. "You know you are welcome any time."

In half hour Mitch showed up at his door and rang the door bell. Richard opened the door and both men walked to the study. When Mitch settled down in his usual place at the sofa, Richard offered him a mug of Sumatran coffee. Love of specialty coffee was a trait both men shared.

"This is good stuff, just picked it up at a store down in the Ithaca Commons a few days back." said Richard sitting down across from Mitch in an easy chair.

He could see a government vehicle parked outside that presumably brought Mitch to Ithaca, Richard thought to himself. Plus the face of his friend looked somber, so Richard knew this was not a casual visit. His friend clearly had something on his mind.

CHAPTER 7

Since 9/11, the U.S. government had pumped billions of dollars into Pakistan. It was done overtly through various aid bills passed by the Congress and also covertly using secret conduits and shell companies and even via some foreign governments. The Iran Contra affair was a distant memory. The language of 'You are either with us or against us', did not leave much room for anyone to argue. National security was the one and only mantra in Washington and who would dare oppose a President in times of war? The war started by the brutal attack on the homeland?

The suddenly resurrected friendship between the two countries was not mutual or even real for that matter. It was a matter of mutual need. The Pakistanis had long felt ignored, even snubbed by their cold war masters whom they had served well during the Soviet occupation of the neighboring Afghanistan. *After all that we did, the Americans should pay far more attention to us,* was the common feeling among the Pakistani elites and especially among the army bosses, the de facto rulers of that nation. During the Soviet occupation of their neighbor, Pakistanis, on behest of the Americans had systematically developed a loosely knit fighting force of *Mujahedeen*. *Taliban* were one of the groups that emerged from that era. Fostered by active encouragement of the ISI with funds from the United States, the *Taliban* had become a formidable fighting force that eventually contributed to the downfall of the Soviets in Afghanistan.

However, a lot of water had passed under the bridge since then. Old loyalties based on mutual convenience were suffering from new harsh realities. The new administration in the U.S. was showing a far better, nuanced understanding of the geopolitical realities in this part of the world, no doubt shaped by the international exposure of the new young president. General Chaudhry was not too happy how events were unfolding around him. Phrases like 'Afghan-Pakistan strategy' were in Washington's vocabulary which infuriated him. To be coupled with the backward, war-torn neighbor to the West was not what he and others like him appreciated.

The audacious American raid in *Abbotabad* had devastated army's morale. The killing of Osama bin Laden from right under the nose of the army was deeply humiliating. Whatever American funding that was trickling in would surely stop or would be coupled with an onerous verification regime. There was one bright spot in all this, if you could call it that. He was approached by a mysterious American who had promised generous help in return for something. General Chaudhry didn't like dealing with a nameless, faceless partner. But what other options did he have really? This mysterious man could bring the necessary funding in the time of financial crisis. The general was very uncomfortable with the blind phone meetings with this American. He was particularly disturbed since the last scrambled phone call he had received from the American a week ago.

General Chaudhry sat down in a plush chair in his home office. He was partial to the decorations of the colonial era. His office reflected his taste. Ambience of his office could have fooled somebody to believe they were in the early twentieth century England. The floor was made from teak hardwood and polished to perfection. The furniture consisting of elegantly designed mahogany desks and chairs was a mélange of British and Indian styles. Huge wall paintings adorning the pastel colored walls were again a strange mixture, showing scenes from an English countryside fox hunt to Rubaiyats of Omar Khayyam. The room looked like a smoking room from one of the British estate homes. It was a hangover from his younger days in England, the days filled with dreams and ambitions. He wasn't particularly happy where the fate had brought him though.

"*Salam Alaikum.*" the unknown voice greeted him from the other end.

"*Alaikum Salam.*" said General Chaudhry.

He was suddenly irritated. He found it condescending for non-Muslims, especially Westerners to use the traditional greeting. Educated in England, he was fluent in English; in fact he believed he could speak better, more cultured English than the Americans. But they were the masters of the universe.

Bloody stupid, he said inaudibly.

"Have you thought about what we discussed last time?" queried the unknown voice.

Of course the general had thought of it. In fact he was so consumed by what he had heard, he had not been able to sleep, or enjoy the gourmet meals cooked by his chef; even the fine single-malt scotch remained untouched the entire week.

Yes, I have thought about it alright, you fool; he said to himself and cleared his throat to speak.

"Yes, I have given it careful consideration. However, I am not yet ready to take it up with the General." replied Iqbal Chaudhry.

The reference to 'the General' was meant to be the head of ISI, and both parties of the conversation were obviously aware of it.

"We don't have a whole lot of time brother." said the Yankee cowboy.

It took general Chaudhry to another level of irritation. He did not like to do business with this particular person. But this contact was made through a very reliable old friend now serving in Pakistan's embassy in Washington D.C. And the proposition alluded to by this Yankee was most unusual. It made general Chaudhry both excited and fearful at the same time.

Unknown to the two parties, there were two other individuals listening on the call and one of them was recording it with highly sophisticated, state-of-the-art telecommunication gear.

CHAPTER 8

The national elections in India, now almost three years old, had given a strong mandate to the Congress party, the largest partner in the ruling coalition. Ever since the elections, the Indian National Congress party was tightening its grip on power. A pro-growth agenda was considered a sure thing for the next five years. The nuclear deal between India and the U.S. looked to be on solid ground, making the large U.S. businesses happy. It had taken sheer persistence and unfolding of new realities in the sub-continent to bring about this deal. Many arms were twisted. In India it was done almost openly in the Parliament, sometimes with public humiliation. Internationally, the horse trading took place behind closed doors in influential capitals and at the offices of the International Atomic Agency.

Since the early 1990s, India had relaxed its policies with respect to foreign investment. It had opened up its doors albeit cautiously, to the world, on the backdrop of nearly forty years of socialist ideology. There had always been family based business conglomerates in India, but now they and other professional entrepreneurs were free to play on the world stage. India was eyeing to be counted as one of the Asian Tigers.

U.S. based large businesses were keenly aware of the changing business climate in India, especially since the early 1980s, when the flow of skilled and cheap Information Technology labor had started migrating to the U.S. mainland. These bright young boys and girls from the best Indian universities were a harbinger of the IT outsourcing tsunami that was to follow. Massive foreign exchange inflows generated by the IT services industry had transformed the beautiful garden city of Bangalore into the Indian equivalent of the Silicon Valley. And the story was repeated across other cities like Hyderabad, Pune, Gurgaon and Noida. And of course India's financial capital, the city of Mumbai saw a fair share of the IT related growth as well. This IT expansion had made new billionaires, both in India and in the U.S.

These businesses had acted as a catalyst that spurred the wave of outsourcing from the U.S and European countries. The emergence of a new country as a force to be reckoned with was not a new phenomenon by any means. In the 1960s and beyond, the Japanese had gained a substantial foothold in exporting manufactured goods to the U.S. Their early products were derided and considered to be of lesser quality, but soon Toyota and Honda learned and created a powerhouse that became known for the top quality of their products.

Now China was in a similar early stage of low margin, low quality manufacturing, although at an unprecedented scale of operations. India's English speaking, skilled workforce had given it an early mover's advantage in the high paying white collared jobs such as financial analysis, radiologists, tax preparers, IT research and development and so on. Any U.S. or European company of any size could not compete without an 'India strategy'. It was the vindication sought by the free market proponents of how global growth and prosperity is helped by the free markets. Investment communities everywhere loved it and they sent stock prices soaring.

Was everything just right and hunky-dory? Well not quite.

As in any economic boom there are winners and then there are losers. Some lose due to their inability to see an opportunity and seize it. Some just see sour grapes in spite of their own success, simply because they couldn't succeed even more. Roger Patel was an example of the latter. He had created tremendous wealth riding on this outsourcing wave, yet he had missed out on some of the key areas of the emerging technology and was not positioned competitively in those areas. Even the thought of not being in the top three among competing businesses frightened him.

Visionaries saw the emerging importance of clean fuel alternatives, nano-technology, genetic research and embedded systems that were becoming smarter and pervasive in all walks of life. Roger Patel was ambitious, daring and opportunistic, but he was not a visionary. His companies had not made the strategic investments needed to gain a strong foothold in these new avenues of wealth creation. He had ridden the IT wave far too long and had rested on his laurels while others had outsmarted him. And that made him furious.

And then there was the country of Pakistan, the twin sibling of India, but the sibling that followed a path of religious zealotry and was left in the dust by her slowly prospering twin. General Chaudhry and his ilk did not take very kindly to the unfolding of events over the past two decades. The global forces of prosperity had skirted around their country and landed next door. How many times had his country tried to woo the American businesses to establish IT presence in Pakistan only to be disappointed by their lack of confidence in peace and stability? It was a bitter lesson that lack of a stable democracy does not provide a foundation required to attract business capital.

There was yet another group; a group consisting of protectionist conservatives in the U.S., that eyed every outsourcing business deal with fear. Although the outsourcing was a broad phenomenon encompassing China, Mexico, and the Eastern European countries like Poland and Hungary, India was a suitable whipping boy in the eyes of these groups. Opposition to *mango diplomacy* and references like *macaca* had become part of rhetoric in the previous U.S. elections.

CHAPTER 9

S id's flights were on schedule. His parents dropped him at the Birmingham-Shuttlesworth airport. He had a connecting flight in Philadelphia which brought him to the Ithaca-Courtland Regional airport, from where it was a short fifteen minute ride to the campus. His friend Tony picked him up at the airport and they drove straight to Collegetown where a bunch of friends were gathered in a bagel sandwich coffee shop, a local favorite.

"Hey guys, how are ya'll!" Sid greeted the crowd gathered around a table in the bagel shop.

Sid had formed a close knit group of friends at Cromwell. His friends came from various parts of the college with common interests in academics, athletics, various clubs he participated in and some just became friends around the campus. They all made fun of him as a Southerner although Sid didn't have Southern accent. He however played the role and usually used the Southern phrases on purpose. His 'ya'll' almost sounded like 'yawl' that amused his friends. Sid ordered a latte and sat down in the narrow opening next to Sarah. They hugged and Sarah queried.

"So, how was your spring break at your parents?"

That was another point where his friends made jokes in good jest about Sid's close family ties. While most college kids spent spring break at more youthful places such as at beach or with friends, Sid had insisted on going home for his final spring break. He was thinking of accepting the job Professor Levine had talked to him about. And if he did that, there will be no time left to go home after graduation.

"It was great, relaxing." said Sid.

Sarah Johansson was a junior in the College of Arts and Sciences, majoring in Economics and International Trade. They had been dating for almost one year. The two had met at a hockey game through some common friends and had taken instant liking to each other. They both enjoyed jogging and hiking when weather permitted, and were constantly in each other's company through various club activities. They even studied together although their course work was completely different. Sid often teased her about how easy it was to be an economist because no two economists ever agreed with each other and both would be right most of the time.

Sid had an apartment off Dryden Road. Sarah was a couple of blocks away on the same street. Both were runners. Sid had developed a habit of running since the days of his lacrosse training. Although he wasn't on a team since his junior year in college, his passion for running was still strong. He would run with Sarah at least two or three times a week. Their favorite route was to start from their respective apartments, to College Avenue, over the foot bridge and onto the Orchards. They would typically cover seven or eight miles each run.

They both had run couple of half-marathons together. Although Sarah had not played any team sport, she was involved in track and field in her high school. One hundred meter hurdles was her favorite event. She was athletic by nature and had developed liking for running from her high school days. The fact that they both liked each other's company was obvious to all their friends. Their dating was perhaps going to survive the college days, but it was too early to tell. Besides they were both quite busy to think much ahead in future.

The conversation around the table was lively as usual. But Sid's mind was drifting away to the talk he had with Professor Levine.

CHAPTER 10

Sid loathed parting the company of his friends gathered at the bagel joint, especially Sarah; but he had an appointment to see Dr. Levine.

Ever since he took a computer cryptography course in his second year at Cromwell, Sid was totally impressed by Professor Levine. He was unlike any other teacher Sid had had in high school or college so far. Sid found Professor Levine to be a strict teacher and a task master who knew his subject inside out. The assignments and class quizzes were difficult and the tests were excruciatingly painful. But at the same time there was something about Professor Levine that made the torture of learning the subject very agreeable.

The hallmark of a good teacher is to provoke his students to meet challenges in front of them and guide them to conquer the challenges without spoon feeding. Professor Levine did all that and more. His was an inspiring presence both in the classroom and in his office where he met students with an open door policy. Sid had made full use of the opportunity to learn from the great mind, spending many hours in professor's office while other students were happy to learn just enough to pass a test.

It is said that an ultimate reward for a teacher is to find a deserving pupil. Professor Levine had come across many bright students during his teaching career and he was a good judge of a student's potential. He found in Sid both a great potential and mental tenacity combined with very easy going, polite demeanor. Sid had asked for more and

Professor Levine had very willingly provided more. It was as if the two had a private tutoring relationship that took Sid far beyond the coursework, well into the masters or PhD level work. Needless to say, Sid was Professor Levine's favorite student. The close bond between the teacher and the student was going to last well beyond the college years and they both knew it.

So it was not a surprise when Professor Levine called Sid during winter break and told him about a job that paid well and would provide Sid with a path towards a great career.

"No, this job is not posted with the placement office." Professor Levine had said.

"It's a great opportunity but it's somewhat unusual." he had added, raising Sid's curiosity.

"Why don't we discuss it before you take up any other offer? Make sure you see me right after spring break", Professor Levine had continued.

Sid had known about Professor Levine's consulting role with various government agencies and with corporate clients. He had sort of surmised the nature of the job to be with a clandestine agency in the U.S. government. Sid had often thought of serving his country since the high school days where the armed forces routinely ran recruitment drives. But he didn't find a career in armed forces very appealing. There must be a better way to contribute, he had thought and had moved on.

Sid put his arm around Sarah and held her close. Sarah feigned to lose her balance and fell in his arms. Sid held her close for a while, but realized it was time to go see the Professor. Sarah showed her displeasure by squinting her eyes in mock anger as Sid helped her sit upright and got up.

"See you tomorrow at the foot bridge." she said, as Sid got up, referring to the Trolley Foot Bridge, the meeting point of their cross country running course.

It was exactly 5 p.m. when Sid knocked on the office door in Rhodes Hall.

"Come in." Professor Levine shouted over the sound of Jazz album he was listening to while reading a research paper.

As Sid entered, Professor Levine put down the reading material on his desk.

"So, how was spring break?" he asked while turning off the music.

"Oh, it was relaxing." Sid replied, taking seat in one of the visitor chairs.

"My parents were quite happy I did visit home, and I sold my motorcycle." Sid continued.

"That's splendid." mumbled the professor.

Sid could sense his mentor transforming into a more serious mood. Professor Levine cleared his throat and continued.

"Now Sid, I want you to know that there is absolutely no pressure from me in what I am going to share with you. As you know I do some government work from time to time and happen to know a few people in right places. That is, in right places to benefit my best students."

Professor Levine readjusted in his seat, took a sip of water from a glass on his desk and continued.

"You know in our business, the best goddam thinking doesn't mean a thing unless you can apply it somewhere."

Professor Levine paused for emphasis and then continued.

"And you have certainly reached a level where you are going to need some extraordinary resources to harvest that brain of yours. You with me?"

Sid gave a polite nod. However well he knew the professor, it was still a little awkward to hear flattery from him. And there couldn't be any better words to boost Sid's ego than what he just heard in an off-the-cuff remark from the professor. Professor Levine leaned forward on his desk, looking Sid in the eye and continued.

"And you know who's got the best toys when it comes to computers and security, right? It's Uncle Sam, Sid."

Sid had not heard Professor Levine speak in this manner before.

"And Uncle Sam has your and my tax dollars to work with, so they can afford the best there is. And the starting salary isn't bad either at around $80K per year."

Sid took notice and perked up. The average salary of a Cromwell Computer Science graduate wasn't that high.

"Of course there is no free lunch as you know." The professor said rocking back and forth in his chair.

"Uncle Sam expects a lot in return for what is offered. It's not an easy job, but then knowing you, you never settled for just easy anyways." Professor Levine chuckled as he said this.

The professor talked for the next fifteen minutes or so and Sid was in rapt attention. A few students passed by the office, peeked in through the glass opening in the office door and saw Sid get up and pace the narrow space in front of Professor Levine's desk. Outside, an impromptu game of Frisbee had started in the quad and the excited students could be heard faintly inside the office.

Sid nodded several times and looked engaged in a two way conversation. The mentor and the mentee were engrossed in verbal exchange for about hour and a half.

CHAPTER 11

Sarah was a vivacious young lady. Her sweet nature and almost flawless looks belied the somewhat difficult childhood she had to live through. Her dad, Bob Johansson had passed away when Sarah was three years old. Cindy, her mother had raised Sarah and her older sister. Bob was a certified public accountant in a small practice in Minneapolis. Cindy was teaching middle school when Bob was killed in a terrible car accident. Cindy had moved to Kansas to be near her family and had raised her two daughters there; working two jobs at times to supplement the modest insurance payment she received.

But Mrs. Johansson was resolved to one thing, which was to see her daughters learn and do well in life. And that's how it was done. Cindy never married again, devoting all her attention to the two daughters. Sarah and her older sister graduated near top of their high school classes and had secured admission in prestigious universities. Sarah had landed in Cromwell with a full scholarship and Cindy was immensely grateful for the financial assistance from the university.

As Sid left the bagel place, Sarah could sense something unusual about him. Sid looked preoccupied with some thoughts. The two usually shared what was on their mind as close friends do. After one hour or so the group of friends started to thin down, and Sarah excused herself too. It was a short walk to her shared apartment. The evening air was crisp and getting a little chilly. Sarah, the track and field athlete, had a spring in her step as her shoulder-length, free flowing hair bounced. She quickly made a pony tail and tied it up without a break in her stride.

Her roommates were still away on break and would not return for couple more days. Sarah sat in front of the TV and turned it on, only to switch it off in less than a minute. She picked up her phone from the couch and thought of dialing Sid's number, but after brooding over it for a few seconds decided against it. Just then her phone buzzed. It was Sid. Sarah's face lit up as she pressed the talk button.

"Hey there, what's up with you?" she queried trying not to show any concern in her voice.

"I have a job offer Sarah." Sid got right to the point.

"Are you free for dinner? I want to get your take on something."

They had met over dinner many times before, but never had Sid asked her out in this tone. Somehow it sounded quite grown up. *Oh my god, I hope he doesn't propose or something,* she thought. Even though they had been dating for a while, the subject of taking it any further had not come up so far. She wasn't sure she knew how to react to the topic if it came up. She knew that she liked him a lot and that he was fond of her as well. But a college romance was one thing and getting a job and starting a new life was something else entirely. Besides she had one more year before her graduation. She suddenly felt tension in her jaw.

They met for dinner at an Italian restaurant that was usually a little out of their budget. But Sid had a job offer and thought he could buy a nice dinner for both of them. Soon after antipasti, Sid told her of the job offer.

"It's with the CIA." he said in a hushed tone.

"What?" Sarah just burst in laughter barely managing to keep her food in her mouth.

"You're kidding me, right?" she finally managed to say.

Sid looked uncomfortable and gestured her to be quiet. He didn't want any unwanted attention, as if he already was working for the spy agency.

"No, I am not kidding, Professor Levine has this inside track with a higher up in CIA and they are looking for someone like me." Sid said, while breaking a piece of garlic bread with his hands.

"They want me to join immediately after graduation and most likely move out of the country for a year or so", he continued.

The laughter drained from Sarah's face and she looked anxious. She knew that Sid wouldn't be on campus after graduation in a few more weeks, but the fact that the job offer was a done deal made Sid's departure very real and imminent. Besides being away from the country would certainly make it that much harder to see him, she thought. She quickly regained her composure and asked.

"So what will you do for the CIA? Kill some bad guys?"

Sid shrugged and said, "No, you silly! CIA also needs bright young computer science graduates to figure out who the bad guys are and what they are up to." he said.

He further explained that the job was not a part of the routine recruitment. It was filled only by personal invitation by a select few experts that CIA depended on. The job would involve field training for close to one year, usually somewhere in Europe, but it could be almost anywhere in the world. After one year, he would be stationed in Virginia and will only occasionally need to travel. The job would involve scenario modeling on supercomputers making some very advanced theoretical work an implementable reality. As he explained, Sid's face lit up with excitement.

He talked for a while, as Sarah just stared at him, transfixed. The words sounded like coming from a distant echoing chamber. Sarah felt embarrassed how easily she got emotional and lost control of herself, albeit very temporarily. She snapped out of her reverie.

"Congrats Sid, well done." she said and on an impulse leaned forward and kissed him warmly on cheek.

Sid leaned forward, held Sarah's hands in his and looked into her eyes. He thought he saw a hint of tears.

"Well, this means I won't see you for a while, huh?"

Sarah tried to sound casual, but the words came out hoarse as if she had cold. She cleared her throat fighting back unknown, strange emotions. It wasn't like her to get all mushy and sentimental. She had always been tough, self-reliant and in control.

"Can you come visit me? How often would you be able to come back?"

She was having hard time figuring out what was going on in her own mind.

CHAPTER 12

When stealth is the essential characteristic in its charter, how the heck can Congress effectively oversee it? Representative Pete Osborne was known to have said this of the CIA on more than one occasion. And if anyone, he would be in a position to know. Peter J. Osborne had been a ranking member in the Intelligence Committee of the House of Representatives in the United States Congress.

As he knew so well, leading CIA was not an easy task, but it was a necessary task that he would carry out with utmost integrity. The new president had just appointed Pete to the position of the Director of the CIA. The confirmation hearings were swift and only a matter of routine. After the massive and systemic failures uncovered by the events leading to 9/11, the administrations, both past and the current had placed heavy emphasis on running the spy agencies well. Being able to connect the dots was of paramount importance.

Peter J. Osborne was an accomplished trial lawyer in his early career before he decided to enter politics. Solving a case and defending his clients was an intellectual challenge he had taken on numerous times. When he entered the House of Representative, his natural inclination was towards law and justice matters which eventually led him to the House Intelligence Committee. Pete had shown a thorough understanding of the very complex issues of international power struggles and had understood the nuances of international diplomacy. Both were factors that drove the nation's spy agency.

That is to say that both these issues along with the national security should have driven the CIA's operations.

But Pete had been around the block many times. He knew full well that a large organization like the CIA tends to assume a life of its own and metamorphoses into several fiefdoms led by either corrupt or partisan bureaucrats who have their own agenda.

He often talked sarcastically during his speeches on the floor of the House of Representatives.

"Thanks for all the taxpayer funding and the cloak of covert operations. Yes, thanks indeed. Now we know what's best for America and we'll give it to you."

He was referring to the philosophy of many in the CIA and Pete had decided not to tolerate such rogue elements after his appointment.

The famous CIA lobby at the Langley headquarters was filled with high level CIA personnel and of course the ubiquitous press. Director Osborne was to make an important speech, the first public speech of his tenure after having taken control of the agency some eight weeks ago.

Mitch Shelby found his way to the lobby twenty minutes before the speech was to begin. One of the CIA initiatives he was charged with was about digital security. Mitch was obviously one of the most qualified people either inside or outside the CIA for the job. His superiors knew it and they had given him a large budget and a free reign to develop the initiative into an effective program that would keep the homeland safe and competitive. Safeguarding the homeland was not a new territory to Mitch. He had crystal clear ideas on how he would do it. He had specific ideas that he wanted to implement in order to complement the existing work in this area. But this bit about the competitive advantage was nagging him. It was a political tightrope balancing act that he would have to perform. In the labyrinth of the CIA, NSA, Pentagon and a few other secret agencies, there had been strong cross currents of dogmatic thinking to take a more active role in these matters.

The argument was that, after all, America's competitive advantage was de facto a prerequisite of its national security.

Numerous examples were cited by these individuals where foreign governments actively supported their industry in defiance of the WTO guidelines, which obviously hurt the U.S. businesses.

"Terrorists use bombs and missiles to accomplish the destruction they seek. But don't underestimate what some loosely knit Mafia groups or even some sovereign governments are capable of in way of industrial espionage that'll hurt us big time."

Oliver Martin had said this to Mitch when the two met a few weeks ago. Oliver was a very influential thinker and strategist in the Pentagon's own spy unit. It was well known that Oliver had tacit support of many at the Pentagon including the past Secretary of Defense. The seat of dogmatic thinking was traditionally very strong at the Pentagon. Oliver was the spokesperson and a provocateur at the nucleus of that faction. And he was influential.

Mitch worked his way through the growing crowd towards Freddie Solomon, the station chief for the Indian sub-continent. The two had a lot to talk about. Mitch's elite communication encryption technician had stumbled upon a strange conversation with obvious links to Freddie's sphere of influence. Although Mitch couldn't share how he got the information, he felt it was imperative to share it with Freddie.

While the new director was addressing his employees and the press, a powerful but informal caucus was in progress at the Pentagon. The four men in Oliver Martin's office were in civilian clothes, but they projected power and authority as if they were the joint chiefs.

"So Oliver, what's your read on this Mitch Shelby?" One of the silver haired gentlemen asked.

"He is smart, no doubt. And he is shrewd, knows his stuff and he is definitely a Washington insider." Oliver replied.

"That's a powerful combination." opined another gentleman.

"We don't want a seasoned insider in that position unless of course it's one of our people." The same man continued, chuckling as if he said something funny.

Oliver opened a document on his computer and read excerpts from it. The document was a file on Mitch Shelby. It must have been put together in a hurry as it was a little incomplete. They discussed it for ten minutes or so.

One of the men lighted a cigar. He got up and walked to a window so as not to offend his fellow co-conspirators.

"We have to shake up things a little, over there in Asia." He said between taking puffs of his cigar. From the sound of his delivery, he was obviously the leader of the group.

"Well Oliver, I don't need to spell it out to you." He continued.

"And we may not need a lot of funding either if we play our cards right. Although I admit that an infusion of non-traceable cash will go a long way with these bastards. They don't trust the Swiss any more after our foolish treasury cracked down hard on the Swiss banks."

"I'll keep my ears open and nose to the ground. If there is anything afoot anywhere, you know I'll smell it." Oliver Martin said with hint of pride in his voice.

It was not unlike a hound dog pleasing his master.

CHAPTER 13

The four storied glass building in Mountain View, California looked small from the outside, but it was spacious from the inside. It was the world headquarters of Pinnacle Systems. The company employed around 30,000 staff worldwide. The headquarters building itself had the support staff such as human resources and accounting. The top floor of the building was exclusively for executive personnel. Roger Patel had the northeast corner office. His office was a fairly austere workplace unlike what one might expect of an almost billionaire. The office was a reflection of how Roger ran his business, in a frugal, tight ship manner with a no nonsense attitude.

His office environment, however, belied of his personal lifestyle, which was a mixture of lavishness and simplicity all at once. Roger lived a simple, solitary personal life. Unlike other executives of his stature, he didn't employ a large domestic staff. He didn't throw lavish parties or mix with the social elites. On the other hand Roger owned several expensive cars, couple of yachts and had exclusive access to a private jet. The airplane was of course owned by his company as a business necessity to take him on his numerous trips. He owned a house in Mountain View, a penthouse on New York's Park Avenue and a luxurious four bedroom apartment in Washington D.C., the last being his latest purchase made almost one year ago. Roger had been taking many trips to the nation's capital of late and coincidentally had become somewhat of an introvert, the fact not missed by his executive assistant Lisa Morgan.

Lisa was a quintessential executive assistant. She was intelligent, discreet, trustworthy and extremely efficient. It had never been an easy job to manage Roger's schedule over the past ten years or so since she took up the position of his personal secretary. Pinnacle Systems had seen phenomenal growth, thanks to the very favorable market for the outsourcing business in general. On top of the favorable conditions, Roger drove the top line growth aggressively, expanding his business to all continents.

"Roger, you have several messages from Walter." said Lisa as she brought in a cup of hot cocoa for Roger.

It was 5:30 a.m. Pacific time and Roger, as usual was at his desk. Walter Hastings was the company CFO. Roger had made some imprudent acquisitions of late and surely his CFO had the usual lecture to chastise him of the consequences.

"Screw him." he blurted out.

"And get me the Wall Street Journal and print me the next quarter forecast for the emerging line." said Roger.

And then as an afterthought he added, "please".

He knew when he was irascible and made amends by adding 'please' every now and then when he asked Lisa to do something for him.

After nearly two decades of explosive growth, the business was not growing as fast as it once did. The stock market had readjusted the P/E multiple downwards. It was not willing to pay a premium anymore for the Pinnacle System stock. The heady days of stock options and getting richer by day were behind him and for the investors in his company. Roger's board of directors had a good representation from the venture capital company that had helped him get started. They were visibly displeased of late and Roger himself was not happy with his own performance.

The outsourcing business was a numbers game. The more you shaved off the labor cost in India, Poland and Chile, the more it would contribute to the bottom line. Pinnacle Systems had a huge presence in the three countries which brought cheap computer engineers to do the meticulous and labor intensive job of programming and system maintenance for many of the fortune 500 companies in the U.S. and similar large businesses in Europe. Cost cutting was the mantra for these large profit-making machines and Pinnacle Systems gave them a cheap alternative to hiring and managing expensive resources in their domestic labor markets.

The thinking was similar to the big three automobile companies setting up plants in Mexico and Eastern Europe to beat the inflated labor costs in North America. Now admittedly, lack of unions in the field of Information Technology made a big difference, but the lower output of this white collar workforce was still a problem for these large businesses. Whereas a computer engineer with a four year college degree would work seven days a week for fewer than twenty thousand dollars per year in India, the similar salary barely got you an unskilled person who worked in a company cafeteria as a bus boy. Besides, the workforce in these countries was grateful to even get that kind of money which resulted in good personal productivity from these eWorkers.

Roger Patel played this numbers game very well. Pinnacle Systems had some type of business relationship with more than half the Fortune 500 businesses. The revenues were steady and growing; that was true until couple of years ago. Competition had certainly caught up from such quarters as traditional platinum names like IBM, Oracle and Accenture. Although somewhat late to the party, these large established businesses had realized the value of setting up shops in the third world countries with large educated populations. They were eating away at the market share of Pinnacle Systems. Besides the lure of cheap eWorkers for immediate 'on the clock' hourly rate-based work, these businesses had also set up an R&D presence in India. And they were reaping big benefits from their investments and vision. Many new technology patents were created in these research labs. Whereas companies like Pinnacle System were counting on the salary differential between the U.S. and other third world countries, the visionary companies invested in nano-technology, high end R&D in the areas of chip design, embedded systems and other non-software industries.

To catch up, Roger had acquired a large company in India engaged in embedded systems for digital signal processing applications. The company was not doing so well, which is why Roger thought he could buy it on the cheap and then turn it around. He had gone against the wishes of his board members in closing the deal just as he had done several times last year, although at a smaller scale. Now the bottom line of his company was adversely affected and Roger had no clear way out of the situation. His board was getting visibly impatient. Driven by extreme competitiveness and without the guiding wisdom and help of a cadre of trusted advisors, Roger was feeling very lonely at the top.

Lisa knocked on the door, bringing Roger back to the present and brought in the Wall Street Journal and the Emerging Line reports.

"Thanks Lisa, that'll be all for now." Roger said rather absent mindedly.

What's eating him up? Lisa wondered as she closed the office door behind her and sat at her own desk. A thin flow of cars was coming in the parking lot and motion sensing lights were turning on in various parts of the building. Early work hours were a curse of the West Coast presence, especially for those working with European and East Coast establishments. Of course working for a demanding boss who was an early morning person himself didn't help either.

Roger started to scrutinize information in the reports and his face darkened. After studying the information in front of him for more than fifteen minutes, he sat back in his chair, took off his reading glasses and gave out a loud scream of disgust and disappointment. Lisa knew better than to open his office door to inquire.

CHAPTER 14

Mitch Shelby's current position was at the highest level he had ever worked. He was division head of the CIA's Digital Security. Mitch had a vast challenge in front of him. There were new frontiers that had emerged in the last few years. A lot of talking heads were discussing these on the non-stop news channels on TV. Mitch had deep understanding of the emerging threats and had several ideas in mind he wanted to put into action.

At the same time, Mitch knew the importance of keeping a step ahead of other countries in normal security measures employed in human communication. Just plain old telex and telephone conversations had been encrypted for several decades by now, using increasingly sophisticated algorithms. The trouble was that such algorithms were easy to break as well. A disturbing trend the CIA had noticed was the involvement of sovereign government organizations that had deployed massive amount of resources to break communication encryptions. Mitch knew he couldn't ignore this issue while he focused on more advanced and newer threats.

Therefore Mitch had formed an elite unit of bright technical minds of 'code breakers'. Reminiscent of the World War II stories of the Germans and the Allies breaking each other's communication ciphers, this unit was charged with breaking any encrypted communication they chose to. Kenneth Pope, the techie supervisor who ran this unit had come up with a unique way of keeping scores and motivating his crew to be on a constant lookout for new obstacles.

He would carefully post a challenge and start a frenzy of competitive hacking among his staff to be the first to break the code. A shrewd manager of people, Kenneth knew what motivated his staff. While it might be a surprise to most mid-level managers in the corporate world, Kenneth knew that recognition among peers was the highest honor to his staff, even beyond any financial reward.

"Sir, we have found something interesting you may want to listen to." said Kenneth in one of their weekly calls. Mitch didn't really want to get involved. There were procedures in place to take care of situation where his folks broke a 'crypto' as they called it.

No communication was sacrosanct to his group and Kenneth often swept communication channels emanating from or terminating within the U.S. government apparatus. Although the CIA had no jurisdiction in the U.S., communication via radio waves and off-shore cables was technically not in the U.S. territory. It was a high score item to break code used by any U.S. agency. The logic of course was that if the code is breakable by us then some foreign spy agency may have already broken it too.

"One of my guys has been following this particular thread for the last month." Kenneth continued.

"I want you to listen to the conversation. It's still in a computer altered voice but I am sure we can restore the natural voices if we work on it further."

Then Kenneth pressed a few buttons on his equipment. Mitch listened intently for thirty seconds or so.

"It sounds serious." Mitch said when the snippet of the recorded conversation stopped playing.

"What are the end points?" Mitch asked.

"This is the best we have been able to gather so far." Kenneth replied.

"It's somewhere in the Pentagon complex at one end and somewhere in Southern Pakistan, UAE, Southern Iran or the East Coast of India at the other end." Kenneth paused for his revelation to sink in.

Putting together the end points of this secret conversation would most certainly lead to a high score hit. Kenneth was sure of that.

Besides, he knew that the matter was way over his head as a code breaker and he needed to escalate it.

Mitch was silent at the other end. Kenneth waited patiently. After a long pause Mitch spoke.

"Can you further pinpoint for me the end points?" Mitch conveyed in his voice that it was not an option.

"Especially the one in Asia or the Middle East? For reasons you can understand, it's a game changer and I want to be certain of who is talking to whom. And thanks for bringing it to my attention."

"You're welcome sir." Kenneth replied.

"We are working on this and as soon as we get any further, I will keep you posted."

Mitch Shelby hung up the phone and looked at the wall clock in his office. He still had half-hour before his next meeting. Whatever this conversation was, it was not his business. But he must alert somebody about it. Of course he needed concrete, specific information before he would even know whom to pass it on to.

Three Weeks Later:

"Sir, we have a breakthrough!" Kenneth Pope's excited voice came through Mitch's phone as he picked it up.

"The case we talked about, remember the recording I played for you?" Kenneth couldn't hide his excitement. It would be a nice feather in his group's collective cap.

"Yes Kenny, I remember it. So what have you been able to find?" Mitch asked.

Mitch had been waiting to hear from Kenneth Pope. This was a loose end he would have liked to tie up quickly and make it someone else's problem. He had plenty to do already.

"Well sir, the geo code was hard to break, but my guy figured it out. The far end is in Karachi, Pakistan. And yes, we have been able to work on the computer altered voices too."

Kenneth was going to go on and on, but checked himself in time. He would have loved to describe in detail how they figured out all this while working round the clock, patiently watching the channel for the next conversation. But he knew Mitch was busy and would appreciate a summary instead.

"We intercepted this conversation just minutes ago. Would you like to hear it now?" Kenneth asked. He knew what the answer was going to be and had placed his finger on the right button on his rather complex equipment to play the recording.

"Sure, put it on." Mitch said and listened. The recording started to play.

Voice 1:

"Yes, I have given it careful consideration. However, I am not yet ready to take it up with the general."

Voice 2:

"We don't have a whole lot of time brother. I am a patient man general. But you know I can't wait forever. Sooner or later the deal will be off. I hope you have seen that I deliver what I promise."

Voice 1:

"And we certainly appreciate your goodwill gestures. Your delegation was most accommodating and we all thank you for that. But what you are asking is worth a whole lot more and you know it. We are not some cheap dogs you can throw a bone at and expect lifelong loyalty. It's going to be bloody expensive for you."

Voice 2:

"And I don't give a rat's ass as to what you think. The offer is on the table. Take it or leave it. But if you turn me down without even mentioning it to your general, I can't guarantee your own people will take it too kindly when they know. May Allah save you."

As the recorded snippet of conversation ended, Mitch looked quizzically at the phone. Kenneth spoke.

"Sir one of the voices is unmistakably an American, most likely someone from the Southeast."

Mitch nodded in agreement.

"The other voice, as far as we could ascertain is that of an Indian or a Pakistani male with a British education. Of course knowing the end point of Karachi, sort of narrows that down."

Kenneth couldn't hide from his voice the sense of accomplishment he felt.

"Well done Kenny. This is certainly very important and disturbing piece." Mitch meant every word he said.

"Package this and everything else you got along with your analysis and ready a drop for me. I'll let you know soon who the lucky soul is to pick this up and run with it."

Mitch hung up after giving a few more instructions and words of encouragement to Kenneth Pope. After all, a valuable staff's sense of pride and accomplishment must never go unrewarded without the proportional praise. Mitch knew his people and he was very appreciative of what they did.

He tapped his fingers on his clean, neatly organized desk.

Looks like I am going to be dealing with Freddie Solomon more than I thought. Mitch mused to himself.

CHAPTER 15

R oger Patel was a member of the Software and Information Industry Association. Of late, Roger had been taking an active role in lobbying efforts on behalf of the organization and for his own company as well. He had worked to develop personal relationship with politicians who mattered. He knew well both senators from his home state of California. Quota for the H1B visa was always a matter of intense debate in Washington. Congress had often debated the issue where members on both sides of the isle would perform grandstanding for the benefit of their constituents, but in the end the lobbying effort always worked and the industry got what it wanted.

The last presidential election cycle had brought up the topic of outsourcing jobs yet one more time. Candidates were making speeches against outsourcing, claiming it to be at the root of the nation's declining wages. While that may have been true, the global trend was unstoppable in Roger's mind. He and others in the industry had actively sought out candidates who saw the issue through a lens favorable to the industry. Roger had personally participated in many fund raisers and had donated good amount of money himself. In one of the fund raisers Roger had met Jim Arnold of the Arnold & Gregg, a Washington D.C. lobbying firm.

Jim, with his keen sense of people had immediately chalked up Roger as a potential client with deep pockets. Jim had cultivated a relationship with Roger Patel by turning on his personal charm and the apparatus of his resourceful firm. Jim had created a file on Roger and as was his routine, he periodically opened the file scrutinizing it for any leads. The firm's accountants had uncovered some troubling facts about Pinnacle Systems. There were notes in the file explaining financial difficulties of the company in layman's terms. These notes were of particular interest to Jim. It seemed that Pinnacle Systems had made many acquisitions in the past three years and the synergy that was expected from the new businesses was just not to be found. The acquisitions had piled up a mountain of debt without the increased revenue and cash flow that was expected. Servicing of the debt was still not an issue because the tax laws allowed Pinnacle Systems or any business for that matter to write off interest expenses and capitalize part of the acquisition cost, thus generating a valuable tax advantage.

Now this is where it's getting interesting.

Jim Arnold was talking to himself. He pondered for a while and then dialed an extension.

"Joe, I need you to get me the C-SPAN recordings of the H.R. 19623 proceedings and get dossiers on all the major players as well."

Joe was the librarian, the research assistant, and a go-to person for all matters related to the legislative proceedings. Jim knew he would have all the details in half an hour.

Jim walked to the bar in his office, poured himself a generous portion of bourbon over ice and sat at his desk. He was meeting Roger Patel the day after tomorrow at the Software and Information Industry Association or SIIA briefing. But obviously he must meet Roger separately, he thought, and sooner the better. He picked up his Blackberry and in few keystrokes found Roger's private number and dialed it. Jim adjusted the earpiece of his hands-free while the phone was ringing and took a sip from his drink.

"Roger, this is Jim Arnold, how are you sir?" said Jim in his specially cultivated voice.

Like a good salesman Jim had learned to modulate his voice and express what sounded like a genuine interest in the party he was calling. His deep baritone provided the gravitas that put a caller on notice of a no nonsense, no frivolity setting. Listeners got a sense of trust and comfort or they were plainly intimidated, depending on the words Jim would use. He was of course speaking in a friendly manner in this conversation. He waited for Roger's response and continued.

"Roger, there is a bill in Congress that I think would be of some interest to you."

"Would you like to discuss it tomorrow at the club? I think your CFO will approve, what's his name? Walter somebody or the other."

Jim knew very well who the CFO was and had all the pertinent information on Walter Hastings in Roger's file. There must have been silence at the other end because Jim continued.

"You there Roger?"

Roger Patel was thinking at the other end. *This guy Jim Arnold must have a sixth sense or something,* Roger wondered. Because his CFO had been calling and leaving messages on precisely the same topic.

Well I guess I better find out what this is all about, Roger thought and spoke in his phone.

"Yes Jim, I am here. There are just too many balls in the air right now." Roger was thinking as he spoke.

"But I suppose we could meet tomorrow evening at the club. I touch down in D.C. around five thirty Eastern, so I'll go directly to the club."

The club they decided to meet at was Blue Pearl, a frequent hangout of Washington D.C.'s movers and shakers. Jim was thinking fast. His cunning mind was in overdrive. There were several things coming together nicely, he thought to himself. That is if he could play Roger Patel in the right way. But he had to activate Todd Lester to pull in the other side of the deal he was designing in his mind.

It's about time to activate Mr. Lester. Jim murmured to himself.

He concluded his conversation with Roger Patel after customary pleasantries. Soon afterwards, his thumbs got busy again.

"Todd, I want you to come up to my office." He said.

"Can you do that in the next ten minutes or are you tied up with something?"

"Well okay, see you in five." he said and hung up the phone.

There was just enough time for Jim to enjoy his bourbon.

CHAPTER 16

Professor Richard Levine and Mitch Shelby sipped their coffee, appreciating its rich flavor. A true coffee connoisseur never gulps it down, not because the coffee is usually hot, but because you can't really do justice to a good coffee unless you enjoy its aroma. In the case of Dr. Levine, a nice cup of coffee was usually followed by a few puffs at his pipe stuffed with his favorite tobacco.

Professor Levine finished his coffee and turned to the Briar pipe on his coffee table. He methodically cleaned the pipe and started packing it with the lightly scented tobacco he stored in a pouch. He had been through this ritual many times but while he was focusing on all this he sensed Mitch's body language as Mitch shifted uneasily in his sofa seat.

Professor Levine looked at his friend's face and decided to cut down on the preamble to the real discussion his friend had come all this way for.

"Well Mitch, what's on your mind? You certainly didn't come here in your armored vehicle to enjoy my coffee, now did you?" Professor Levine asked.

While the reference to an armored car was just an attempt at levity on part of Professor Levine, the truth of the matter was that Mitch Shelby's car was indeed a bullet proof, government issue vehicle driven by a chauffeur who was better at weapons handling and hand to hand combat than he was at driving.

"No Richard, you are right. I certainly appreciate the coffee. But as you so rightly guessed, I have a request for you." Mitch said. "You know that I have assumed a lot more responsibility under our new leadership at the agency. I had no idea how complicated and multi-faceted this business of digital security is, truth be told. I won't bore you with all the details and quite frankly I can't say much as you know."

Mitch spoke while readjusting himself in the sofa, his favorite spot in Richard's house.

Apart from their personal friendship, or perhaps because of their personal relationship, Professor Levine had occasionally helped Mitch in recruiting bright young talent into the government sector. Some government jobs, especially in high tech areas of the secret service agencies, could not be filled very easily by job placement advertisement in New York Times. And these were well paying jobs with a patriotic angle to them. Besides, deep pockets of the Federal government meant that the jobs usually involved state-of-the-art equipment and a 'pushing the envelope' kind of mindset that could be very rewarding to the right person. The last student he recruited was Sid Joshi, one of the brightest and easy going mentees of Professor Levine.

Professor Levine looked at the serious face of his friend and listened for a while. Apparently a lot of bad folks were trying their utmost to figure out how to breach security of servers in various sensitive areas of operation both inside the U.S. government and in key industries. The usual targets such as power plants, nuclear facilities, power grids and so on were on the hit list of these cyber criminals. There was nothing new or unusual about it, Richard thought.

What was causing Mitch to stay up at night was not any of the above. There were enough experts handling all the angles and then some more. Of course he couldn't go through the classified information and Richard understood. Mitch had often joked about spilling out classified information.

"Look Richard, I can tell you this and that, but then I'll have to kill you." was the standing joke between the two friends. And

Richard would always replay, "Oh what a cliché, can't you do better than that?"

But on the more serious note, the latest intelligence picked up by the United States was raising an entirely new set of threats.

"Richard, we are looking at a Trojan Horse multiplied by a billion, give or take." Mitch explained.

A Trojan Horse was obviously a well known modus operandi of hackers to gain an entry into a secured area by hiding inside an overtly innocuous object. Professor Levine, an authority on computer cryptography and security knew all about it.

"This threat is different." continued Mitch Shelby. He meticulously outlined the problem as an academic would do.

The modern industrial infrastructure depended on pre-fabricated components that were manufactured in many different places of the world. Manufacturing or building something complex often involved assembly of hundreds of thousands of such components. Mitch gave an example of the infamous episode of the U.S. presidential helicopter. Some years back, the U.S. press had broken a story of how the contract for the Marine One fleet included several key components that were manufactured by companies owned by foreign governments.

"Just imagine if some unfriendly governments pressed their manufacturers just enough to include say a secret listening device in the components they manufacture." Mitch explained.

"Worse still, what if they engineer something to fail when an external, coded signal is received? What would be the consequences?"

It was obviously a rhetorical question. The unfortunate slip regarding the Marine One contract was of course corrected immediately by the U.S government once press broke the story.

Mitch continued.

"Now think about all the embedded systems we burn into chips and smart components these days. Everything from a small mobile phone to an aircraft uses hundreds of thousands of these components with embedded software burned into them. Many of the more advanced components allow maintenance engineers to update the flash memory by downloading a later version of the software from the OEM website, often without involving any security steps."

Professor Levine grunted his concern. The problem was now obvious to him and his mind was already racing through the various permutations of potential safeguards and counter measures that he would come up with, only to be foiled by the attackers by circumventing the safeguards. It was the old cops and robbers game played like chess moves in his mind.

Mitch noticed the contemplative frown on his friend's forehead and paused. He knew Richard had understood much more than what was said and had leaped through many scenarios and counter scenarios. This was precisely why Mitch liked his friend's company. Conversation with Richard was never repetitive or redundant. For someone who lived in the Washington D.C. bureaucracy, these conversations were like a breath of fresh air.

But this was not a problem solving session and Mitch was short on time. Mitch interrupted his friend.

"I am sorry Richard, let me stop you right there. We believe we can't solve this problem. At least not in the time we have. There has to be another solution."

Richard looked at Mitch quizzically raising his right eyebrow. He had not taken any puffs from his pipe and the tobacco was barely lit anymore.

"We believe the only way we can prevent the onslaught of terror attacks we are afraid of is to declare a trade embargo against suspect manufacturers operating in countries outside of the U.S. We will find some excuse to declare the embargo, but the trouble is we have no definitive knowledge of whom to target."

Mitch was now sounding a little shaky. He cleared his throat and continued.

"We know for a fact that India houses some of the high-end embedded systems development centers in the world. That is the place of origin where some miscreants wishing to do us harm will focus first. Now we are sensitive to the political realities and while India has not been our closest ally all these decades, we understand that it's a democracy that wishes us no harm. But in my business

I get paid to be suspicious and treat people as guilty until proven innocent."

Professor Levine was somewhat taken aback. He had never heard the edge to Mitch's voice as he was witnessing just now.

"What are you saying Mitch? Are you insinuating what I think you are?" Now Richard's voice had a little edge on it too.

He had numerous colleagues of Indian origin, all fine scientists and he was sure they all were very loyal to their new country, the United States of America. He had also travelled many times to the elite educational institutes in India for lectures and scholarly exchanges. Mitch saw the turmoil in his friend's eyes. He bent forward touching Richard on his left forearm.

"Richard, unfortunately it's very convoluted and let me assure you I don't want you to do anything that makes you uncomfortable."

The bright noon was giving way to long shadows outside. The two friends were huddled in Professor Levine's study almost for an hour. To a distant observer, the body language of the two told the story of what was transpiring. Mitch was leaning forward, tapping his fingers on the coffee table and gesturing with his hands. Richard looked uncomfortable and skeptical as evidenced by frown on his forehead. Finally Richard sat back looking relaxed, his hands tied and supporting his neck as he reclined in the sofa chair.

Mitch pulled out his communication gadget, pressed a few keys and in a minute his driver walked up to the study door carrying a briefcase.

"This has everything you'll need." Mitch said as he handed the briefcase to the outstretched hand of his friend.

"You know your boy as well as anybody. He and his unit are at your disposal. The agency will take care of all planning, logistics and resources on the ground. You have to let Brad Malone know how you want to proceed. And of course prep your boy Sid for what's expected of him. And remember I am only a phone call away. You have my private number. And again, Richard, I am so thankful for your help."

Mitch had finished what he had come all this way to say. He hated to burden his friend this way. But he didn't know who else to turn to. Mitch smiled as they shook hands.

It would be a short drive to an unlisted military airstrip nearby where a small plane was waiting to take him back to Langley.

Richard Levine slowly got up from his chair. He felt like there was a tremendous weight placed on his shoulders.

CHAPTER 17

Todd hung up the phone and looked like the weight of the world had been dumped on him. Ever since joining the firm, Todd had worked hard, completing many assignments where he had provided information privy only to a select few in the Pentagon. Most of the cases had involved defense contractors seeking specific inside information or an angle on biases of an individual who would be making a call on certain large contract and so on. There were some cases related to foreign parties, whose details were not disclosed even to Todd, which made him somewhat uncomfortable.

The firm of Arnold & Gregg was extraordinarily adept at obfuscation and compartmentalization of processes. Information was shared with the employees strictly on a need to know basis. There were several briefings Todd had received from senior associates of the firm after which he had walked out more confused than when he entered, but with just enough information to carry out his individual task. Todd was a Washington insider and as such, he wasn't naïve to know why his work was organized this way. It was a clever setup to protect the firm from leaks and to also provide deniability to its employees if there ever was an investigation. In the twenty five year history of the firm, there had been some close calls, but never an inquiry or investigation. That would be bad for business.

Todd was getting a feeling that Jim wanted him to do more. It would certainly make sense. Todd was very well compensated. But for the life of him, Todd could not put a finger on exactly what he was expected to do beyond the assignments he had been working on. So when he got this phone call from Jim, Todd was certain the time had come for him to deliver. He pulled his sizeable frame up from his desk, straightened his tie, patted down his hair and let out a sigh.

He didn't need to carry anything. The firm had easy information access from almost anywhere in the building. When your business depended on digging up information, sometimes at a moment's notice, you had better be set up to do just that. That's how the founding partners had thought from day one, and had invested in the required information technology infrastructure and talented staff to run it. Of course Todd's real value was not locked in an information database in a computer. His deep knowledge of the Pentagon, accumulated over the decades he had spent there, was stored in his head.

Jim had just finished his drink when Todd knocked on the door and entered. The office was huge, befitting a CEO of a large corporation. The floor was covered with thick luxurious carpet and adorned by exquisite imported Persian rugs, effectively dividing the huge room into smaller virtual enclaves. These enclaves were of various sizes as defined by the furniture set up, from two person privacy setup to an elaborate glass and metal conference table that could seat twelve. The conference table was surrounded by a soundproof clear glass enclosure making it a private area even though it looked like part of a huge office. Every sitting arrangement had its own thin, unobtrusive computer screen and a few mini bars were not too far against the glass walls. The conference table was equipped with a state-of-the-art video conferencing system.

"And what's your pleasure, Todd?" Jim asked as he walked to the oversized bar that took major part of one of his office walls. Todd knew better than to decline, so he said "How about Glenmorangie straight up?"

"You got it." Jim said as he motioned Todd towards the conference table. Todd was a little confused. He didn't see anyone else and couldn't quite figure out the need for the conference setting. But he walked towards the glass door, opened it and took a seat at the center of the table. Jim followed with two crystal glasses and placed them on the table.

"What do you know of arms supply to Pakistan?" Jim asked as he sat down next to Todd.

"God knows we give them enough of everything. Enough to even meet any asymmetric threat. But they never stop complaining." Todd replied.

Todd started to search his memory. He was involved in negotiations with the Pakistanis on many occasions, usually as a subject matter expert to the State Department. Traditionally, the Pakistan strategy was always run by the State Department except in the days of the Soviet occupation of Afghanistan and the early days after 9/11 when the Pentagon had taken up the lead.

"Well, Jim what do you want to know?" Todd asked as he picked up his glass. "To tell you the truth, we in the Pentagon don't like to deal with the Pakistanis. They always want more and the latest but they very seldom cooperate when we want something from them."

Jim nodded and said, "Yeah I know, like that tall bearded Arab they were harboring over there. But that's beside the point. Tell me about the army head honchos you have dealt with over there."

Todd had had experience with many of them on his trips to the region and he could list their names and personality profiles easily. Over the next half hour, Todd spoke, only occasionally interrupted by Jim to clarify something. Jim was making notes on a writing pad. This was unusual. Normally Jim would have a junior analyst do the job of taking notes.

This must be something big, Todd thought.

Jim got up once to get a refill for both of them. His sharp mind was never dulled by alcohol consumption, but rather stimulated by it.

"How well do you know Oliver Martin?" he asked when they were almost finished. This was a sudden departure from the chain of conversation so far. Todd was surprised by the switch.

Jim knew of Todd's conservative views and had guessed that if he didn't know Oliver Martin directly, Todd would at least know someone who knows Mr. Martin. It turned out that Todd knew

Oliver Martin personally although they were not close by any calculations. Todd was about to formulate a reply when Jim spoke.

"I want you to arrange a telephone meeting between Mr. Martin and a client of ours." said Jim. "Let me know when you can do it."

Todd stumbled a little. "What's this about?" he asked.

He was thinking. You don't just summon up Oliver Martin without declaring an agenda and parties he is going to meet with. Jim looked irritated.

"Just tell him it's to do with America's competitiveness and some such bullshit. I don't know. Just get him on the phone for half hour and I'll do the explaining." Jim spat out an order.

Todd knew the meeting was over and he took leave of his boss. *There we go again*, he thought. *Yet another blindfolded runaround in a maze.* He was stressed out and his mind strayed to the business card the lovely angel had left by his pillow the morning after the Blue Pearl party.

CHAPTER 18

Mitch Shelby was feeling uneasy. Over the years of working in secret organizations of the U.S. government, he had developed a sixth sense of sorts and it was telling him something was afoot. He was getting chatter about a new set of threats. These threats had to do with the embedded system parts that were assembled in myriads of finished products. As if he didn't have enough other issues to worry about. Mitch had never personally thought too much about the subject and therefore had reached out to his trusted friend Professor Richard Levine.

Mitch knew that Richard would get to the bottom of the various threat scenarios that can potentially emanate from embedded systems better than anyone else and would create a clear, credible picture of the threats as well as their respective countermeasures. Mitch was also gathering intelligence about some scientists collaborating with anti-US elements to design and build embedded system parts that could sabotage sensitive infrastructure in the U.S. His talk with the station chief of the Indian subcontinent had added to his anxiety as the possibility of a rogue scientist was also echoed by Freddie. This certainly created a sense of urgency for Mitch. He was contemplating some plan of action in the India context. Again, his friend from academia was the one who he turned to for help.

Mitch needed a bright computer security expert, preferably of Indian origin, and who better than the young recruit, Professor Levine's protégé, who was already working for the CIA. Mitch had pulled Sid Joshi's file and although he was still in the first year of field training, the situation demanded that he be pulled out of the training for this assignment. Mitch had talked to Brad Malone and had put the plan in motion. This of course was far different from the type of things Brad would normally handle. So again he had asked his friend from Cromwell University to figure out how best to use Sid.

Mitch hated putting such burdens on his friend, but he had no choice. Besides, this was almost a civilian assignment to get to know the brains behind India's embedded system design might. Once that was accomplished and the players were known with certainty, the regular CIA could take over the job. Mitch was happy that he had set the right strategy in motion. He put his hands behind his head and reclined in his office chair, stretching his aching neck and shoulder muscles.

A right combination of brain and attitude were Mitch Shelby's strongest assets. He was also hard working and fiercely patriotic. What drove him was his pursuit of perfection and the love for his country. He didn't have much patience with the corporate ladder or the government bureaucracy. However he had found the right vocation as a security expert, both in and out of government. He had worked as a freelance security expert for many years, but the CIA job was what suited him the best. He had a much larger sphere of influence and could therefore accomplish much more for his country. What Mitch wasn't prepared for was the political tap dance which he would have to now perform in his new position.

Since he assumed his new role, people had come out of the woodwork. They came from everywhere to vie for his attention, no doubt with naked self-interest in mind. He could ignore or handle most of them, but Oliver Martin couldn't be shrugged off. In fact, Mitch was to meet Mr. Martin at the Langley cafeteria for lunch. It was flattering that Mr. Martin would come all the way from the Pentagon to meet with him.

Oliver Martin was quite ordinary looking to those who saw him from distance. However, anyone who met Oliver and spoke a few words with him would know immediately that this man was no ordinary soul. His sparkling but cunning eyes impressed anyone in close range not unlike a cougar staring at you. He had an engaging style of talking. From his intelligent and clever arguments, it would be obvious that Oliver Martin was a thinker, a preacher and a provocateur. This was their third meeting and Mitch didn't really want to meet. But he flashed a smile and extended his hand when he saw Oliver at the entrance to the cafeteria. As usual, Oliver was pontificating to a small group of followers who were cherishing every word that came out of his mouth.

"Ah, there you are. Well gentlemen, I must take your leave now to see this important man." Oliver addressed the group and winked as if to underscore his sarcasm with the notion that Mitch was of any importance whatsoever. That was quintessential Oliver Martin.

They both went through a rather short lunch line at this early hour and sat down at a corner table.

"So, I hear you have dispatched somebody already to attend to our concerns in India?" Oliver queried.

Mitch was taken aback. Sid had still not left the U.S. Besides Sid was handpicked and handled through Richard Levine. How did Oliver know about it?

"It's imperative we stamp out any problems at the earliest and at the same time promote domestic manufacturing. We have a boatload of very fine universities you know." Oliver was on his soapbox again.

Mitch shrugged a non committal response, not confirming or denying anything. It was the Washington staple diet taught in Politics 101. But Oliver pressed on.

"The Indians and the Chinese think they can bully us with the population might they possess. The lure of cheap labor will die soon my friend, and then what will happen?"

"An entire generation or two in the U.S. will have completely lost any notion of how to survive in this new world. They wouldn't know how to produce anything or how to program the complex systems we use."

Mitch had to agree with some of the points Oliver was making, but Oliver's assertive style, dismissive of any counter criticism and a preacher-like *I'll tell you what God wants from you* stance was irritating.

"The Chinese dump their prison labor manufactured goods at our door and the Indians have cheapened the information technology cost where we just can't compete. And the ironic thing is that our universities are churning out most of our future competition." Oliver continued.

The last statement was referring to the fact that most U.S. universities enrolled a disproportionately large number of Indian and Chinese students in scientific and advanced-technology coursework.

Throughout lunch, Oliver Martin freely spoke what was on his mind. Mitch was sufficiently numb from the onslaught. That's when Oliver said something that got Mitch's attention.

"And in the spirit of inter-agency cooperation, while your boy is there, we would like him to find out some information for us."

Then Oliver lowered his voice to a conspiratorial whisper.

"There is a secret location where the Indians are developing a specialized chip that's going to, shall I say, put us at a competitive disadvantage?" He paused for effect. "And we have reasons to believe that this secret project is housed in one of the private commercial companies engaged in the outsourcing business."

Mitch was irritated to a level he couldn't tolerate anymore. He was also angry as a result of what he had just heard.

"Wow, wait a minute Mr. Martin. First of all I would like to find out how the hell do you know whom I am sending where and for what purpose? In the best interest of our inter-agency cooperation, of course." Now Mitch was showing his sarcastic side.

"And besides, I don't run my people to execute someone else's plans. This operation, and I am not willing to discuss anything further except this, is strictly a low risk, low footprint endeavor that I am running to cover certain angles." Mitch said strongly and then turned more conciliatory. "I can perhaps accommodate your request, but I need to know everything you know first. And then I'll, solely at my own discretion, make a call if I want to play or not."

Oliver Martin's face turned red as he gritted his teeth. When he spoke, the venom in his eyes was clear as daylight, but the words came out chillingly casual.

"Well Mitch Shelby, I thought we had an opportunity here to cooperate and gain synergy. But as I see it you don't want to play ball. That's quite alright. Have a good day."

And with that Oliver Martin got up and stormed out of the cafeteria.

Mitch grunted a sigh and got up himself. He had to deal with this complication now, whether he liked it or not.

CHAPTER 19

Every day, newspaper headlines were shouting out the news of violence. TV channels showed nothing but footage of daily carnage in some parts of the country. The Taliban was proving to be a multi-headed demon that just wouldn't go away. You shut it down in one place and it would manifest itself somewhere else. The North-West Frontier Province was as unruly as ever and the unrest was spreading to the Punjab and Sindh provinces as well. It was looking like Pakistan's strategy of supporting terrorism while lip-singing in support of America's war on terror was backfiring. The traditional play of crying wolf of Indian aggression was not working anymore. Opinion polls were clearly showing that majority of citizens were just tired of the bloodshed and were not willing to blame their easterly neighbor for the anarchy.

General Chaudhry was pacing back and forth from his home office to the living quarters of his huge Karachi home. His orderly, Yusuf Gilani, was having a tough time keeping at a discreet distance from the General, should he call for him. A lot had transpired since the last time the Yankee had called. General Chaudhry was sensing an internal turmoil. The worst kind of nagging is when it comes from within. Lately, Iqbal Chaudhry was experiencing a lot of that.

Yusuf watched his master from a distance. Yusuf was devoted to serving his master. The only time Yusuf was his own man was when he prayed on his mat, five times daily. Yusuf found a deep sense of fulfillment when he prayed. He left the house only to go to a mosque and to buy supplies for the General. Since the General's wife had passed away some years back, Yusuf had been running the household. He obviously didn't approve of the General's weakness of giving in to alcohol, nor did he approve when the General entertained his colleagues and tolerated occasional serving of pork in his house. But the General was his master and Yusuf would serve his master well.

General Chaudhry had a call to make. The Yankee who spoke over the scrambled lines had proved to be true to his words. In spite of the lynch mob mentality in Washington D.C. against his country, the money transfers were made as scheduled. Surprisingly, the Pentagon delegation visiting Islamabad had agreed to favorable terms and conditions. And as verified by his people, the CIA operative was on the ground in Pune, India.

General Chaudhry didn't trust the Americans. But he had to admit that at least in this case, they were holding up their side of the deal.

The ISI had an extensive network of spies and informants in India. Perhaps financed by various alleged activities such as currency counterfeit operation, drug smuggling and nuclear proliferation, the ISI could simply buy information. It could also influence certain people by fanning the religious sensitivities that are ever so present in India, just under the surface. The General had verified that the CIA man was indeed mobilized and was in the process of gaining access to key establishments.

So why was he feeling so uneasy? He wished Allah would give him a clear conscience to do what he must. But unfortunately he was not receiving the guidance he so desperately wanted. He was at a cross roads in the choices he needed to make. What seemed like a destined path didn't feel like the right thing to do anymore. Was he getting weak in his older years? Or was he seeing the wisdom he had refused to see all this time?

An hour passed and the General kept looking at his watch every few minutes as if it would make the time go faster. It was time to dial the scrambled line and reach this irritating Yankee for the final time. The General let out a grunt and marched towards his office.

This time he would initiate the complex dialing procedure himself without help from his orderly.

"*Salam Alaikum*" the voice greeted him.

This time General Chaudhry simply ignored the greeting and got directly to the point. "We have a deal, but only for an authentic but empty container. As agreed, the container will be traceable to our friends in the Far East, but we will not load it under any circumstances."

There was a perceptible silence at the other end. The General had surprised himself too by turning away so resolutely from the earlier understanding. "If what you desire is indeed what you say, then I don't see why an empty container will not do." he pressed on.

The scrambled voice resumed over the line. "Sure, as you wish. It's a deal. When and where will the delivery be made?"

General Chaudhry was hoping for this answer. He was visibly relieved. "My people will get in touch with your people. This scrambled line will not be operational anymore, so please destroy your codes."

And then as an afterthought he added "Have a good day."

Yusuf hung up the parallel phone he was listening on in the adjacent room and hurried to the General's office just as the General called out his name.

"Get me a double in my bedroom. And prepare the car. I am going in to the city tonight." the General said as he walked out of his office towards his residence.

CHAPTER 20

Symbiotic Research Labs was a behemoth corporation. Its seventy thousand employees were scattered over all the continents. The company had started as a source of cheap labor for outsourced Information Technology work like so many other companies in India. But the vision of its founders had taken it far beyond the low level development and production support work.

Twenty years after its fledgling beginning, the company was a pioneer in the fields of chip design and manufacturing as well as Artificial Intelligence equipped multipurpose robots. The company had research labs and office complexes in all the major Indian cities. The chip design research lab and the manufacturing plant were based just outside of Pune, nestled in the rolling hills of the *Sayhadri* range. The company had selected Pune for its temperate climate, a steady supply of educated workforce, and the tax breaks it received for establishing operations there.

The Pune research and design campus consisted of eight large buildings named after famous Indian scientists and mathematicians. In addition, there were two large conference centers that had auditoriums built for large and small events. The research lab was staffed with the best scientists and engineers from across the globe. Many came to be back in their homeland, but there were many of non-Indian origin as well, who came for a stimulating work environment, good pay, and to visit a country with several thousand years of history. The salary was competitive on world scale, which meant it allowed one to live a very comfortable life in India. With a large supply of household help, almost all daily chores work could be offloaded, leaving the company employees plenty of recreational time after work.

The manufacturing unit was located twenty five kilometers away towards the town of *Talegaon*. Scientists from the research labs routinely visited the manufacturing facility. The company prided itself in a very rapid concept to completion innovation cycle. It necessitated a seamless transfer of knowledge where researchers and manufacturing engineers had to collaborate.

Symbiotic Research Labs had complex working relationships with many leading companies in the U.S., Korea, Europe and Japan. Most of these companies were Symbiotic customers but a few were collaborators in the design and manufacture of specific product lines. Often times its collaborators or customers were fierce competitors of each other. As a result Symbiotic Labs had meticulously created security systems and processes so as to create what corporate circles called a 'Chinese Wall', between the organizational units engaged in competitive interests. The security measures included advanced biometric devices and the creation of each worker's profile that was linked to an artificial intelligence program which learned an individual's work pattern and idiosyncrasies. For example, the system captured the pressure applied by an individual when placing a hand on a fingerprint device. Any significant variation in the pressure would trigger an event that a security expert would have to look at and resolve.

The campus was surrounded by small hills on three sides and had a walled fence all around it. It was secured by modern devices to detect any breach of the perimeter. The security measures were in place mainly to satisfy the foreign customers and collaborators, to assure them that they would not be harmed by industrial espionage.

Anand, Sid's driver, picked up Sid every weekday morning and drove him to the Symbiotic campus. Every time Sid entered the campus, he was amazed by its sheer size and the number of people it employed. The campus usually buzzed with energetic young employees scurrying around from building to building. Some would be out on the lush green lawns, engaged in animated group meetings with their laptops open. The campus looked more like a brand new university rather than a big corporation. The company was also experimenting with several green energy pilots. In addition to altruistic motives of saving the planet, such initiatives saved the company energy costs, thus improving its bottom line as well. The company had installed convenient, priority parking for bicycles. Although commuting to work on bicycles was not practical to any employee, using bicycles to move within campus was encouraged, and Symbiotic Labs provided a few hundred bicycles for this purpose. There were several nature areas where employees could ride bicycles for recreation as well. With Sid's credential as a Crypto Tech scientist, he had relatively free access to the facilities on the Symbiotic Labs campus. No doubt the CIA had pulled several strings, but Crypto Tech had a clout in the universe of embedded systems design and had close working relationship with Symbiotic Labs.

Sid was in close touch with his mentor, Professor Levine and had actually started to enjoy his work as a chip design scientist. Symbiotic Labs had created extensive design and manufacturing processes that were proprietary. This intellectual property was obviously a competitive advantage that helped the company maintain its position as a leader in innovation.

As far as Sid could tell, all the top scientists employed by the company were just professionals, hardly of the inclination to cook up some nefarious plot. But it wasn't his job to make that judgment call. He was just supposed to shortlist names he believed were in a position to potentially plot something or be coerced into such a plot. Sid was sure he'd be wrapping up the assignment in couple of months.

CHAPTER 21

Roger Patel's private jet landed in Washington D.C. He was dressed in business attire. He stepped out of the airplane and walked directly to the limousine that was waiting for him. The call from Jim Arnold had unsettled Roger. But then again, the company he ran was a public corporation and listed on the New York Stock Exchange. This meant that all the financial data was available to anybody who wanted to look at it. And anyone with resources and a will to find out internal details of his company could do so relatively easily. Putting together a financial picture of Pinnacle Systems wasn't that difficult. What was troublesome to Roger was the fact that his company was in the cross-hair of someone like Jim Arnold.

Roger was an office bearer of the information technology industry group. He had met Jim a few times before in this capacity. Roger had found Jim to be a very capable lobbyist, always delivering on what he promised and alerting the industry group of impending events that could potentially adversely affect its members. But at the same time Roger had formed a somewhat negative opinion of Jim Arnold. Roger was a savvy businessman. He often depended on his gut feeling to evaluate a person before striking any business deals. And his instinct was telling him to be cautious.

However, Roger also knew that he had to do something for his company's sagging bottom line and flat growth rate. Even if he held a substantial percentage of Pinnacle Systems stock, he didn't have much time to turn the company around before his job as the chief executive came in danger. In this era of newly found conscience on part of many board members, no doubt due to the post Lehman Brothers financial meltdown that brought the U.S. to the brink of a disastrous recession, his own board of directors and the CFO had become vocal.

Damn it, Roger said in disgust as he loosened his jacket button before sitting down in the luxurious limo.

"To the Blue Pearl." Roger addressed the limo driver.

"Sir, I have been told to take you directly to see Mr. Arnold at his office." the driver replied.

Roger was startled. He noticed it wasn't his usual driver whenever he came to Washington D.C.

Lisa must have goofed up, he thought to himself. He was just reaching for his phone when it rang. It was Jim Arnold on the line.

"A thousand apologies Mr. Patel." The glib baritone of Jim flowed across the line. "There has been a change of plan of sorts. The gentleman I was going to introduce to you has a scheduling conflict and it's not possible for him to meet at the Blue Pearl in person. You know how these things go. Why don't you come to my office instead? We can conduct our business by phone from here and then head on to Blue Pearl."

Something in Jim's voice told Roger that there wasn't much of a choice. He hated to be in this position and cursed himself for getting in the embedded chips business by making a very expensive acquisition. His neck was on the line here and it was obviously worth saving, whatever the cost.

The limo stopped in front of Arnold & Gregg office building and Roger got out. In the building lobby a heavyset man was waiting for him.

"Welcome Mr. Patel. I'm Todd Lester, a senior associate with the firm." he said extending his hand.

Roger was led to a private elevator that went directly to Jim's office. Jim greeted them both and led them to the conference table.

"What can I get for you Roger?" Jim asked.

"Some mineral water please." Roger replied.

"And you Todd?"

Todd replied he was okay as he and Roger sat down at the desk. Jim returned with couple of glasses and a bottle of cold mineral water. He continued to talk as he sat down across from both Roger and Todd.

"My apologies Roger, but the gentleman who can help you is rather busy and is available only by phone."

Todd knew very well that Oliver Martin had refused to meet in person and in fact didn't even want to know who he was going to talk to. It was one more case of Washingtonian obfuscation. Design deniability into the equation. Apart from Jim and Todd, the two parties talking to each other were not supposed to know who they were talking to. That was the pre-condition. Jim didn't care. He was going to collect a fat check from the transaction regardless, so he was mainly interested in making sure the transaction did take place.

"Well Roger, before we dial in this gentleman, let me set the stage for you." Jim said. "As I see it you are in a bind due to your sagging stock value."

Jim knew when he was dealing from a position of strength. He was also shrewd to let the other party know, albeit politely, that he had an upper hand.

"I am sure you know the numbers better than I do. And I am also sure you are feeling the heat from your board members." Jim continued to establish the fact that Roger was in a bad situation. "The question is, what are you willing to do to reverse the declining trend of your stock price?"

Jim was good at this cat and mouse game, skillfully sizing and cornering his prey. His demeanor was friendly but his tone said otherwise. The master knew how to tighten the screws yet make it look sophisticated.

Roger was startled by the directness of Jim's question. Ever since Lisa had given him messages from Walter, Roger had just ignored them, not even bothering to return Walter's calls. Roger was a self-made multi-millionaire, and as such knew he couldn't afford to keep his head buried in the sand for too long. When Roger heard Jim's harsh words he looked like a deer caught in headlights. Todd had seen his boss in action many times before, but never at such a close distance. Todd didn't know whether to loathe him or to admire him.

Roger was silent for a few seconds, trying to digest the situation. He was dealt bad cards and had to figure out if Jim had the trump card or if he was bluffing.

"So, what's your advice Jim? Do you have something in mind?" Roger said, keeping an air of self confidence.

"I think I can help you turn the situation around. It may take a year or so, but I am pretty confident the business will turn around." said Jim.

Jim took a sip from his glass of water and then reached for a stack of papers near him. He pushed the stack rather roughly towards Roger. "My advice is to look this over." he said. "This is H.R. 19623, the bill in Congress that will eliminate rather substantial tax breaks your company enjoys right now. As I see it, your last mega acquisition has put you in a deep hole. Your interest payment on the borrowing is tax-free for now. Imagine what will happen if the tax break for foreign acquisitions goes away."

Jim waited a few second. "It will make a sink hole so deep, that our accountants believe you won't be able to climb out of that."

The words came out spreading a chill down Roger's spine. He suddenly remembered the reference in Walter's messages. *Damn it, I should have paid better attention,* he thought. Roger shifted in his chair. His shoulders sagged and his face looked worried. "And you can stop this bill from passing." he said as a matter of fact.

Jim exploded in laughter. "My friend, who do you think I am? God? I can try very hard to stop it if you'd like us to, but there are no guarantees."

Roger was getting impatient. "So what's the fucking point of this meeting here? I thought you had something to offer me." Roger spat out.

The rising temperature in the room prompted Todd to clear his throat to say something. Jim waived his hand to keep Todd from speaking. There was a pregnant silence, and the air seemed still. Then Jim spoke in a soft, comforting baritone. "It so happens that this certain gentleman may have an interest in, let's say stirring up a few things. Shall I say the kind of things that will not bode well for your competitor?"

Roger was irritated by this vague, conspiratorial talk. But he wanted to hear more.

"And you know what? One thing leads to another and another and lo and behold. Pinnacle Systems subsidiary sees a jump in their orders." Jim was gesturing with smooth hand motions for maximum effect.

Todd's head was spinning.

What the hell was Jim saying? Todd had no idea what was going on. He had arranged a meeting between Oliver Martin and Jim. He had wondered all along what in God's name would the two of them discuss. But Jim was not interested in explaining anything to Todd, at least at the moment.

"Interested?" Jim's question was rhetorical. Roger's body language told the story.

They were engaged in what was rather one sided conversation for the next fifteen minutes. Roger sat expressionless for the most part and nodded at the end when Jim asked him something. Jim motioned to Todd who started dialing Oliver Martin's private number on a secured Polycom placed between the three of them.

CHAPTER 22

Sid unlocked the door to his flat. He had had a long day at work. It was a Friday in July and the Monsoon had brought dark clouds over much of the lower half of India. It was muggy and drizzling outside. Sid found weekends in India quite boring. He had made a few friends at work, but none of them were free to hang out. He thought of visiting the health club he belonged to, but didn't feel up to it. He dropped his backpack on the couch and stared out of the window.

How he missed Sarah. His mind went back to the dinner he had with Sarah in Ithaca. He could still feel her soft lips on his cheek. He had thought about it all the way on his long airplane ride to Europe when he started his training and again on this long trip to Mumbai. He had called her several times in the last eight months, but they had not been able to meet in person. It was more than a year since their dinner and Sid felt this urge to be close to her. And it wasn't just that he had a somewhat lonely existence in India. He had had ample time to think of their relationship and where it may go. Being separated from each other gave him time to think it over objectively. He was reaching a conclusion that he really wanted this relationship to not end. But what was Sarah thinking? It was sort of difficult to discuss this by phone, without the immediacy of her person, her beautiful face and those expressive eyes. *Hope this assignment ends soon,* he thought.

Sid decided to check his emails. He had a specially built laptop issued by his division in the CIA. Sid never used that laptop anywhere outside of his apartment, but he always carried it to work and left it in his car, just in case he needed to use it. There were considerable security measures built into the laptop. It was built with special purpose hardware and it ran an operating system similar to a commercially available edition, but modified in certain ways. It was not known outside a tight circle of CIA technicians and security experts that the ubiquitous Windows operating system had a flavor specially modified by the agency experts. It allowed the agency to provide security at the kernel or operating system level to utilize special purpose hardware installed on their computers.

Sid sat at his desk in the bedroom and flipped open his laptop. He logged in, by providing his password and by pressing both thumbs on the scanning device built on either sides of the keyboard. Once logged in, he connected to the cloud via a rather slow broadband connection from the local carrier. Sid had several emails from Brad Malone. All the emails were of course encrypted from point to point and only Sid's laptop could decrypt the message sent by Brad or other official CIA account holders.

Brad wanted to know how things were going and had asked for Sid's secret code to enter the restricted area within Symbiotic Labs. Sid had often shared such secrets with Brad as it was not uncommon for the handlers of the field agents to know these details. Sid chuckled, thinking of himself as a field agent. He then typed responses to various emails.

Towards the bottom he saw a notification of a personal email. Only his parents and a few close friends had this particular email address. Sid had programmed a piece of tunneling code to send his CIA account a notification of any unopened email to this special personal account. He opened a regular browser to check his personal account.

It was an email from Sarah. She had a job offer from the campus interviews and had decided to accept. It was a job with a lobbying firm in Washington D.C. Sid was happy to read her email. After this assignment he would complete his first year of field training and be stationed at Langley, not too far from where Sarah would be.

That would be nice. He smiled as he quickly typed a response congratulating her.

On an impulse, Sid put his laptop in quiescent mode and got up to go out for a beer. He hated going alone to any of the very few decent bars around. So he walked up to a nearby liquor shop and bought himself a bottle of Hayward 5000 beer. Beers in India were generally much stronger than in America and different in taste from the fine European, especially Czech or Slovak beers he used to enjoy.

Upon his return from the liquor store, Sid took the elevator to his floor and as the elevator doors opened he heard the familiar nagging sound of a door shutting down and a whiff of someone crossing the hallway to the stairs. The door of his flat needed lubrication as it made a similar creaking sound.

And what was that smell? He thought. Many people in India, including his driver had the habit of chewing this strange mixture of tobacco and some other scented ingredients. Sid found that smell offensive but had not said anything to his driver. *Just a few more months,* he thought as he opened the door to his flat.

Sid stopped and caught a hint of that same smell inside his apartment.

My laptop! Sid panicked as he raced to his bedroom. He was relieved to see his laptop was still there. But the monitor glow was a little too bright for the laptop to be in the hibernate mode he had put it in. Sid was worried. Thefts of laptops were not an uncommon occurrence and he was amply warned of it by Brad in his briefings. Not that a thief could have gained anything from stealing Sid's laptop. Any improper operation would simply make the machine inoperable and useless to anybody who stole it. But it would have been a hassle to get a replacement. Besides, that would have been very careless on his part. Sid was happy that the laptop was still there.

CHAPTER 23

Yusuf brought the Mercedes around to the front of the house and parked it in the semicircular driveway. General Chaudhry had three vehicles, but he usually preferred the bullet proof Mercedes sedan. The General came out of the house wearing dark sunglasses, an embroidered short sleeved silk shirt and dark trousers. *No doubt he was going to indulge in some carnal pleasures today,* Yusuf thought to himself. This was yet another flaw of his master, a habit that Yusuf didn't approve of.

What Yusuf had heard on the secured phone today was gnawing at him. It all had started more than six months ago, when he had met someone on insistence of his daughter Zarina. He remembered the conversations with his daughter Zarina and her husband Hamid.

"Abajan, agar aap unka kehana nahi manenge, to woh log muze mar dalenge." Zarina had said with tears rolling down her cheeks. She explained to her father that someone was threatening to kill her unless she could get Yusuf, her father, to cooperate.

Hamid had stood behind her eyeing his wife in disgust, for he didn't want her to be helpless and begging her father. Hamid never felt comfortable with his father-in-law. He thought Yusuf was old fashioned and too stupid to see and acknowledge the world around him.

"Rona nahi Zarina. Tum muze badi mussibat me dal rahi ho." Yusuf made a weak protest claiming she was putting him in jeopardy.

Similar conversation between him and his daughter had been repeated a few times. He was torn between love and safety of his daughter and loyalty to his master. In spite of his unwillingness to do so, he had been forced to meet Mohammed. Mohammed's cruel eyes flashed before him. No, he wouldn't let them harm his beloved daughter.

In light of what he had heard earlier today, he must alert Mohammed at once. But his instructions were clear.

"You can't call me on a phone." Mohammed had said. "Always go to the safe house and leave a word with whoever is there and wait. I will call a phone there and we will talk."

Yusuf had met Mohammed only once. But he had routinely visited the safe house and talked to Mohammed many times, especially in the last couple of months since the mysterious Yankee had started calling.

Yusuf swung the car onto the street and muscled his way in the Karachi city traffic. Although the car was not fitted with any official army insignia, it was obvious to anybody on the streets that the car belonged to a VIP. It had a loud horn which Yusuf wasn't shy of using, so navigating the busy city traffic was not so difficult. He drove for a while and turned off the Abdullah Haroon Road into a private drive. The club was just hundred meters along the small road. General Chaudhry got out and tapped on his watch and raised two fingers in air, indicating that Yusuf should be back in two hours.

Yusuf was used to this routine. The club was a favorite spot among the army's top ranked officers. It was a place to unwind, make new contacts or nurture the old ones. Club membership was by invitation only, usually also accompanied by a hefty joining fee and annual dues. Most drivers waited in the limited parking space for their masters. But the security situation in the city had deteriorated significantly in the last year. As a result the club owners had erected an elaborate security checkpoint taking up much of the parking space that was in short supply to begin with. The drivers were forced to park elsewhere and show up when called. This suited Yusuf very well. He could use the time to contact Mohammed.

Yusuf drove back to the main street and took several turns and U-turns to make sure no one was following him. He then drove straight toward the abandoned railway yard dotted with a sprawl of low rise, dilapidated concrete buildings. The narrow filthy lanes were filled with people, mostly young boys, playing an improvised game of cricket some of the time, but mostly looking for trouble.

Yusuf parked his car at a street corner. He knew that no one would dare touch what very obviously looked like a VIP vehicle. As a precaution, he placed the official red light on the roof. The light attached to the brackets mounted on the top of the car. This now made it an official government car. Nobody would dare even come close to it, and certainly not perpetrate any acts of vandalism.

He then walked through several lanes again taking precaution that no one was following him. He entered a building and climbed the stairs to the third floor. He knocked on a door; three slow taps followed by two quick ones. The door opened and Yusuf entered.

Yusuf was quickly frisked for any listening devices. He was then asked to wait in the next room. The room was devoid of any furniture except a chair and a small table with a phone on it. He waited there for almost twenty minutes until the phone rang. "*Salam Alaikum*" Yusuf opened the conversation politely.

Mohammed's raspy voice was impatient. He demanded to know why Yusuf was calling out of routine.

Yusuf narrated the General's conversation as he had overheard on the phone. Mohammed stopped him to ask a few questions from time to time. Then they exchanged traditional greetings and he hung up.

Tonight, Mohammed was especially appreciative of Yusuf's contribution to the cause. He had profusely thanked Yusuf for his service and had promised that Zarina and Hamid would come to no harm. Yusuf was thankful and relieved to hear that.

Yusuf left the safe house and headed back to the car. It was almost time to pick up the General.

CHAPTER 24

Sid wasn't sure, but he had a feeling of being followed. It wasn't any one incident that triggered his suspicion. His routine in Pune was very simple. He spent most of his time at work except on weekends when he would take off on his own on a two-wheeler. He had purchased a motorcycle that sufficed to get around in this crowded city. His driver Anand, didn't officially have the weekends off and was supposed to be available if Sid wanted the car to go somewhere. Sid very seldom had used his driver on weekends. He wanted to give a nice two day weekend to his driver just as he enjoyed a two day weekend.

A few times Sid had gone to Mumbai for sightseeing and Anand had driven him. Sid had a few relatives from his father's side that he wanted to visit in Mumbai, but so far had not done so. There was Aunt Shashi who was his father's cousin. Sid always found it amusing how Indians had a meticulously evolved nomenclature for various relatives. Your uncle's children were considered your 'cousin-brothers' and 'cousin-sisters', many times simply referred to as brothers and sisters. Sid didn't have any siblings and his cousins were the closest relatives he had in his generation.

Since the laptop incident at his apartment, Sid had become alert and had noticed some strangers taking more interest in him. Brad had told him to be always on his guard. In the beginning Sid found it extremely difficult to scan faces around him to figure out any obvious tails he may have. It might have been due to the sheer number of bodies around him at any given point in time. Starting from his arrival at the Mumbai airport, he was in a sea of people. But lately he was noticing the presence of some men that didn't belong to the sea he had finally acclimated to.

Once when he had stopped his motorcycle in front of a shop on an impulse, a car had immediately stopped about twenty yards in front of him causing a massive cacophony of angry honks on the busy road. Sid had watched from inside the shop as two men, rather well built and professional-looking security guards, got out of the car in panic, scanning the road behind them for his motorcycle. On one other occasion Sid had asked Anand to drive him to the Ajanta and Ellora caves, some two hundred kilometer away from Pune. A car had followed them most of the distance. Even Anand had noticed and made a comment. Sid didn't think much of either incident at the time. But ever since he had suspected someone had broken into his apartment, Sid was paying more attention and what he noticed made him nervous.

Sid knew that there must have been at least one other CIA person on this assignment. It was the agency method to have a backup and a check on the agent officially designated for the assignment. Of course this was hardly an assignment in the usual sense. It felt more like an academic exchange program under the tutelage of Professor Levine. But without his knowledge, Sid's thinking was correct. There was a gentleman, much older than Sid, who was visiting Symbiotic Research Labs for an extended stay. He was part of a large team from a European consortium that was funding research and production of several new generation embeddable chips. Scot Meyer had been around Sid for almost a month now, but the two had not met. There was something in Scot's demeanor that didn't quite gel with the notion of a nerdy scientist he was supposed to be. He could have been someone representing some other government perhaps, Sid had thought.

This particular Friday, Sid had brought two rather thick manuals with him in his backpack. Out of boredom, he occasionally brought home some work and worked in his apartment instead of going to the office. The manuals were confidential and filled with proprietary information. It was the intellectual property of Symbiotic Research Labs. No one was allowed to carry the manuals outside the workplace. But what the heck, he could get some more work done and why would anybody object to that?

On his commute home from work that Friday, the backpack was heavy. As a result, its straps were digging into his shoulders. Sid thought back to his days in high school and at Cromwell when he routinely carried heavy backpacks. This particular weekend Sid decided to go to Mumbai on a whim and had taken a bus instead of asking Anand to drive him. He liked to visit Mumbai and just walk around looking for good restaurants. It always brought back memories of his childhood trips although he hardly remembered the directions or details of any places he had visited as a child.

He reached Pune late Sunday night, taking a bus back from Mumbai and then a rickshaw from the bus stand to his flat. Next morning he picked up his backpack and got in the car as usual when Anand pulled in front of his apartment.

CHAPTER 25

Sid was late to work on Monday morning. His car stalled on their way to work, just before they were to enter the highway. Anand opened the car's bonnet to see what was wrong.

"It'll take ten minutes or so for the engine to cool down so I can make an adjustment." Anand said.

There was a small restaurant nearby. Sid decided to go in there and have a soft drink to escape the heat.

Sid thought of calling Sarah. It wouldn't be too late yet on the East Coast, he thought as he pulled out his mobile phone and dialed. Within seconds he could hear Sarah's excited voice.

"Hi Sid, how are you?" she said. There was a lot of noise around where she was. "Guess what, I am taking the metro back from work."

"What? Already working long hours on your new job?" Sid trifled.

He knew the routine of the first several weeks on job would be exhausting anywhere, but especially in a lobbying firm. It was a people job at its core and networking, remembering names, and researching various issues as they came up was expected of all the junior staff. Sarah's major was in Economics and International Trade. The lobbying firm had some of the large conglomerates as clients. These clients usually had many complex international issues and usually wanted the U.S. government to see their viewpoint. Surely Sarah must be busy.

"I am sharing an apartment in Georgetown." Sarah continued.

"What's the name of your firm?" Sid asked.

"It's Arnold & Gregg. I am so lucky to have gotten a job here. Everybody wants to work at Arnold & Gregg." Sarah was excited to share her success. "How is your work going?" asked Sarah.

"Well it's a job you know." Sid tried to be nonchalant. "Maybe couple more months and I'll be done."

"What's that noise around you?" asked Sarah.

The little restaurant was right on a busy street. There were lots of people around, which was a usual circumstance for Sid. On top of that, a small auto repair shop next door had started a pneumatic tool of some sort that was adding clatter to the usual commotion on the street.

"Well, my car broke down. My driver is looking under the bonnet. So I am waiting in a small restaurant having a Coke. There are lots of people around." Sid explained.

"Your driver is looking under what?" Sarah was confused.

Anand was waiving to him from outside indicating that the car was ready. Sid realized why Sarah was confused.

"Bonnet is what we call hood of a car." He explained. "And I need to get going." He started walking towards the car. Sid didn't like to talk on his phone when others were within earshot. He told Sarah he missed her terribly, said goodbye and hung up.

They reached the Symbiotic Labs campus. As usual, Anand dropped Sid just outside the gate and drove to the parking lot. Sid walked up to the gate, touched his identity card on the security pole, and walked through the turnstile. A shrill sound of an alarm startled him. He looked around.

Was it him? A security guard was watching from inside a booth. He just waved and motioned Sid to keep walking. *It must have been a false alarm;* Sid thought and hopped on one of the community bicycles. He pedaled to his office building. Most of his coworkers were already there. Today, a delegation from the consortium's European headquarters was scheduled to visit the campus. Sid reached his cube, dropped off his backpack and headed to the nearest break room.

"Good morning." a voice came from behind Sid as he was entering the break room.

Morning was a busy time as people swarmed in and out for tea, coffee and breakfast cereal. Since Sid didn't recognize the voice he assumed that the greeting was for someone else.

"Good morning, how are you doing?" the same voice came again, and this time there was a tap on his shoulder.

Sid turned around and faced Scot Meyer who was walking behind him.

"Oh, hi, how are you?" Sid said and shook Scot's hand.

"I am fine, thank you. I am Scot Meyer from the U.K. office. I have seen you around but haven't had a chance to meet you." Scot said.

Sid didn't know why, but he didn't like this guy. There was something not right about him, but Sid couldn't pinpoint it.

"So the cargo is here, hmm?" Scot said with a slight wink and a conspiratorial smile.

Sid was totally confused. "Are you talking about the delegation from Paris?" he asked.

The flow of people moving around made Sid walk on as Scot stood in place. He looked miffed and just stared at Sid as Sid moved out of Scot's earshot. He could see Scot's lips move and just shrugged his shoulders in a display of *sorry, I can't hear you.* Scot stood there for a second, turned around and walked out of the break room.

Scot was activated in a hurry for this short assignment. Evidently, the Americans were short on agents and his MI5 unit was asked by someone if they could help for an easy job. Granted, it was unusual for someone in Britain's domestic spy agency to take this on, but Scot didn't know and didn't care. So he wasn't even suspicious when he was told to buy a ticket himself and was handed cash for it.

Scot Meyer was a sleuth. After spending many years as a police officer, handling drunken soccer fans and pub patrons, he had finally gotten a break. The surge of recruitment in Britain's spy agencies after 9/11 had benefitted him in getting a job as a secret service agent. He could speak passable *Urdu* and *Punjabi*, which was why he was selected for an overseas assignment in India. This was his first trip outside of the continental Europe and he loved the idea. His crash course in computer cryptography prior to starting his new position meant he knew all the key terms and their dictionary meanings. He was smart enough to keep any conversation to generalities and drop right sounding words in a conversation. His thick accent gave him some protection as most people in India didn't quite understand him anyways. It wasn't difficult to play a role of a scientist for a short while. But as Scot knew, he didn't have much time before he would be exposed in one of the in depth discussions he would have to take part in. *The cargo should have been here today.* And after that his job would be over so he could get the hell out of there.

Is this chap Sid not on the ball? he thought to himself as he picked up his pace towards Sid's cubicle.

CHAPTER 26

General Iqbal Chaudhry was furious. He paced his office up and down as was his habbit. The ISI internal investigators routinely watched their senior officers and their immediate relatives for any telltale signs of trouble. The intent was to protect the organization from its officers as well as to protect the officers themselves should a family member decide to turn against them for some reason.

General Chaudhry was of course aware of the practice. But he didn't have any close family members. His wife had passed away some years back and his sister was a victim of the bloody partition of British India in 1947. He had no children or close relatives, nor did his wife. He had therefore never asked for reports of this monitoring activity. The General was of high rank for anybody in the ISI to question his loyalty. So when a report of potential risk was raised by the ISI apparatus, Iqbal Chaudhry was surprised and offended.

The file given to him by the internal investigators included many pictures of his orderly Yusuf Gilani in the railroad gulch area, walking away from the general's official vehicle as well as from his private cars. The area was a rundown settlement that was an eyesore for the Karachi elites. But the General knew that it was much more than an eyesore. It was in fact a sanctuary and breeding ground for the misguided religious fundamentalists who very often believed more in their interpretation of the Muslim values rather than the rule of law. He was also acutely aware of the recent gains made by the Taliban and Al-Qaeda operatives in that area. *What was his loyal servant of a quarter century doing there?* The General thought.

General Chaudhry entered his study and locked the door behind him. He removed a few Victorian paintings from the wall and opened a panel directly behind one of the removed picture frames. He put his hand inside and retrieved a small computer disc. His office and the attached room were equipped with surveillance equipment. The disk could hold over eight hours worth of video recording. The recording equipment was activated upon slightest motion or vibrations anywhere in the two rooms.

General Chaudhry walked to his large desk and inserted the disk into his computer's drive. He then typed a long sequence of authentication code, and sat back. The computer screen came alive with a clear recording of him pacing in the adjacent room just a minute ago. He clicked a few times and positioned the video to play forward from about a week ago. The video showed a lot of empty snippets, presumably due to the motion sensing trigger that was set off either by him or his orderly just walking around in the study or the adjacent room. But soon he zeroed in on the time when he last talked to the irritating American.

What he saw was inexplicable.

He saw himself talking on the scrambled line while at the same time his orderly was listening on the parallel phone in the adjacent room. *Why would he do that?* wondered the General. *And more importantly what did he do with the information he gained from eavesdropping?*

This whole affair with the Yankee voice on the phone had bothered him from the time it started. The only reason he had permitted himself to play along was because his dear and trusted friend. His friend, a diplomat in Pakistan's embassy in Washington D.C. had insisted. His friend had cajoled him to play along and score one for the country. As much as the General hated India, he was not at ease with the Yankee proposal. The General knew full well that the CIA had its share of loose cannons. The ludicrous proposal could not be from the mainstream thinking in CIA, he knew that much. But the secretive Yankee had promised and delivered several substantial favors that ISI was grateful for. With the establishment of the new administration in Washington D.C., American help didn't come easily anymore. There were stringent strings attached to everything. So he, General Chaudhry, had decided to agree to the Yankee's proposal in the hopes of more aid to come. But he had watered down what he was supposed to deliver at the last minute. He had struggled with his conscience and was finally compelled to do what he thought was right.

Ever since his dear wife passed away, the General had slowly undergone a transformation of sorts. He found himself taking time to ruminate upon his life. Up until now, he had never felt a need to do that. Whatever he had been engaged in, he always felt it was exactly the right thing to do. He had no children. The loss of the only person close to him, his wife, had Iqbal rethinking of his own mortality. As part of his job, the General was a keen observer of the world events. But lately he had found himself looking at those events through a different lens.

The two Koreas were making conciliatory gestures even though technically they were still at war. Since passing away of the madman in the North Korea, there were renewed hopes and a real chance of reconciliation. Vietnam became unified soon after the Americans left in defeat. Germany had healed and prospered with a vengeance after unification of the East and the West. Iqbal Chaudhry the man, often yearned for his childhood days in and around Delhi. As much as he hated atrocities committed by the Indian side during the partition, he knew deep in his heart that there were equal numbers of such examples from his side of the border as well. On quiet days when he allowed himself some retrospection, which he became prone to indulge in more and more after his wife's death, he often wondered who the real winners had been from the division of India.

Lately, the so called emerging new world order was bringing into sharp focus answers to the questions he dared not ask all these years. The rise of China as a superpower and that of India as a regional superpower was obvious to all. His own nation was on the brink of bankruptcy and the Indians were dragged down by a constant threat of terrorism, real and imagined, emanating from within his country. General Chaudhry often thought that the partition of India was a stroke of genius on part of the British Empire. Their last act of cunning before they had to let go of the hen laying golden eggs was to poison the hen so the eggs would not be as golden as before. With the passing of time, Iqbal Chaudhry was realizing the futility of infighting between India and Pakistan, the two countries that shared so much history and culture. Two brothers, separated, and at each others' throat. *What was the point of all this?*

And that's why he had decided to water down the delivery of the goods to the Yankee or whoever he was a proxy for.

The General looked resigned. He stopped the video. He had seen enough. The question now was how to assess the damage and how to mitigate it. He reached a decision in his own mind. He would not put the ISI machinery into play. This, he would handle himself.

CHAPTER 27

S arah Johansson was discovering what many new college graduates find out. The work at her new job had nothing to do with her major in college, at least so far. For the last couple of months she had not once been challenged on her understanding of economics or international trade for that matter. Sarah was already questioning why she had worked so hard to study these two subjects. Her work to date had consisted of compiling information on Chilean defense, memorizing names of congressmen on the Foreign Relations Committee in both chambers, and keeping up-to-date on all the defense appropriation bills in the committee and in the pipeline. *That's not what they taught me in college*, she wondered.

The last task was tricky and needed lots of people skills. It wasn't that Sarah was not a people person. She was. But she didn't particularly care for the kind of people she had to deal with in this job. There were so many pretences, and such grandstanding and hypocrisy. She was getting to know the political side of Washington D.C., up close. What she was learning was putting into question the very basic concepts of democracy she held as real.

Sarah was a junior staff in the group led by Todd Lester, who was a senior associate at the prestigious lobbying firm of Arnold & Gregg. Their offer was good, and a chance of living in the Washington D.C. area, not far from where Sid would eventually be, was appealing to her. She had parsed many times all the angles of how she and Sid got along. Her conclusion had consistently been that she was certainly very keen on continuing their close friendship that was in the state of a budding romance. Being away from each other had given her a chance to objectively evaluate her emotions. Sarah was a very practical person. Her upbringing, without a father figure in her life, had made her mature beyond what her age would suggest. Mixing objective thinking in an emotional matter still seemed out of place, but she could also realize why it was a good idea. She was almost sure that Sid felt the same way about her. But the two had not discussed it yet. *There will be time for that,* she had thought.

Sarah had also made a mental note to bring her older sister in confidence to get her take.

"Hey Sarah, the boss wants us in the war room." said Rick, an intern from Yale, breaking Sarah's reverie.

Sarah got up from her chair, grabbed her tablet computer and followed Rick. The war room was not actually a room but rather a cozy place tucked away in a corner of the 9th floor. It was an open area, reminiscent of the Internet Web design studios that had sprung up everywhere during heydays of the dot com era. It was where an impromptu work group was formed and assignments were handed out. An invitation to the war room was a guarantee of late hours and pizza for dinner.

Todd was standing up talking on his phone when a small group of junior staff assembled. Todd hung up and clapped his hands to get everyone to pay attention.

"Listen guys, we have until tomorrow 6 p.m. to finish this." He warned his staff. "We need to pull together a report on the embeddable, programmable chip market." Todd paused to make sure they all understood the core of their assignment.

The junior staff was handpicked from prestigious universities. They were carefully chosen to represent a varied and broad spectrum of academic backgrounds. Todd knew this group would crack anything thrown at them.

He continued to explain.

"Find out who designs them, who manufactures them, the relative market share, price points for break even, assuming a recovery period of three years. I want to know if anybody is dumping these chips.

What is the projected total market value of this segment? Are there sovereign funds or governments backing up any ventures? Come on guys, don't look so clueless. Make calls, Google it, I don't care. Reach out to your friends from college, but get me the information." Todd knew how to rattle them to ensure on time delivery.

Then he added. "And by the way I want it broken down by the end use of these chips. Break it down by the civilian demand versus military complex and also by country."

Todd stopped to gauge the reaction of his crew. They were furiously taking notes, some pounding the keyboards of their tablet PCs. And some looked totally dazed. With interns and junior staff, the first year of employment was like hazing. Only a few bright, hard working individuals among them would survive and be hired as permanent staff.

"And call me directly if you have any questions. OK? Dismissed."

Sarah let out a soft whistle. She had a leg up on her competition. She knew just the right guy to call, a computer science whiz kid, as if she needed a reason to call him.

As Sarah walked to her cubicle, she suddenly remembered her plans for the next weekend. It was her mom's birthday. Sarah and her sister had planned a surprise visit home. But she had to ask Todd for a day off on that Friday. Sarah retraced her steps back to the war room. Todd wasn't there. Sarah took an elevator to Todd's floor. His office door was open. Todd wasn't at his desk. Sarah knocked to get his attention in case he was close by.

"Mr. Lester, are you there?" she called out.

As a senior associate, Todd had another room attached to his office. The extra room didn't have glass walls. It was used for confidential briefings for important clients.

Sarah entered the office. The door to the adjacent room was open and the room was unoccupied. Sarah decided to leave a note for Todd. She approached his desk and peeled off a sheet of sticky notepaper from a stack on his desk. She had started to write when she saw a few papers scattered on his desk. There was a lot of scribbling; circles and lines connecting them. Sarah smiled. It was her style of thinking too. Drawing flowcharts helped her think and make adjustments to her reasoning. As she finished her note, a phrase on one of the papers caught her attention.

There were words 'Symbiotic Research Labs' scribbled inside a circle. That name was familiar. It was where Sid was working in Pune, India. She became even more curious. There were other circles connected to it. Sarah followed the lines. 'Pinnacle' was the next circle connected to it. She followed the line in other direction. It led to a circle with the word 'disruption' which led to another circle with letters 'OM' which led to a circle enclosing words 'Pakistan?'.

Sarah was confused. She recognized 'Symbiotic Research Labs' and perhaps 'Pinnacle' which was the name of a company she had come across. But what or who was 'OM'? And why was Pakistan linked to any of this? It just didn't make any sense.

She didn't want to get caught staring at Todd's notes. She quickly pasted her note on Todd's desk and left.

CHAPTER 28

S cot cast a furtive glance in either direction of the hallway to make sure he wasn't visible to anyone. He dashed into the short aisle of cubicles towards middle of the hall and darted into Sid's cube. He struggled with the zipper of Sid's backpack, opened it and grabbed a brown paper bag tucked under the elastic flaps used to keep the backpack contents in place. He looked around and hid the brown paper bag under his jacket. He turned, bolted out of the cubicle and into the hallway where he reduced his pace so as not to attract attention.

He tiptoed the length of the hallway and was about to enter the elevator lobby when he almost bumped into Sid.

"Oh, I'm sorry Scot." said Sid. "I didn't quite get what you were saying there in the break room. Was I supposed to carry something for you?"

Scot's face drained color. His panic was quite evident to Sid. "No, it was nothing. Just a big misunderstanding." Scot said as he quickly stepped into the stairwell almost pulling the door off its hinges.

Sid's instinct told him to follow Scot, but he didn't. Instead he started walking to his cubicle.

Must call Brad and fill him in. Sid made a mental note for himself as he approached a window in the elevator lobby before turning in the hallway to his cube. He saw Scot leaving the building, evidently carrying something under his jacket, as his gait looked uncomfortable and lopsided. His left arm was holding something which bent his torso to the left.

Sid watched until he saw Scot enter the small auditorium where Symbiotic Labs employees met for various occasions. Sid's facial expression changed to that of concern as he walked to his cube.

There were six rather spacious cubes in the isle where Sid's work area was. Although most of the staff was in at this hour, none of the cubes around Sid were occupied. Two out of the six were unallocated and the remaining three were unoccupied because his officemates were away for a conference. Sid entered his cubicle to find his backpack open. He looked in and didn't see the manuals he had placed in there on Friday when he had decided to take the manuals home.

Had Scot just taken his manuals and hid them under his jacket? Sid was confused. The manuals would not have been of any use to Scot and even though they contained proprietary trade secrets, they were hardly worth stealing in this manner. And what was Scot doing in the auditorium? There wasn't anything scheduled there until the day after tomorrow.

Sid sat down, took his laptop out, docked it and turned it on. He decided to look up Scot Meyer using the company's employee locator to see his availability today. He must meet and talk with Scot to find out what was going on. To Sid's surprise the electronic record indicated that Scot was out of the office today. Sid dialed Scot's extension but got a recorded message that Scot was going to be out for three weeks starting today. Now Sid was really worried. He stayed at his workstation for couple of hours and decided he had to go visit the auditorium. He couldn't concentrate on anything. This whole episode of Scot breaking into his backpack to steal the manuals was bothering him. His training at the agency told him to escalate the matter at once. But Sid didn't want to call Brad and report something strange until he had more information. Brad would react harshly if Sid called prematurely before getting the salient facts.

It was getting close to lunch time. Sid put his laptop in the backpack and decided to leave for the day. He took out his phone, pressed the speed dial number for Anand and waited to talk to him. After several rings he heard the beeps indicating no response. By default, the Indians didn't use voicemail. It always bothered Sid but Anand would see the missed call and call him back.

Sid left the building and walked the short distance to the auditorium. There wasn't anybody in the building. Sid entered the building foyer and walked to the auditorium. He pushed open a door. Silence. No lights, no movement. Sid waited for a minute, and then called out. "Hello, is anybody in there?"

No response.

Sid walked out of the building. Anand had not called him back either. Sid was getting a little frustrated by now. He decided to use one of the community bicycles parked outside the auditorium and pedaled his way to the main entrance. All the cars and drivers waited outside in the parking deck. Sid left the bicycle at a stand near the gate and walked to the parking deck after going through the security gate. He was perspiring from the physical activity. In Pune's summer heat, it didn't take much to sweat. Sid got a handkerchief out of his pocket and wiped his temples and neck.

The parking deck was six stories if one took an elevator or a staircase. But there were almost eleven parking levels crammed into the six stories, making use of every foot of vertical space to pack as many cars and two wheelers as possible. The parking levels were color coded.

Sid had no idea where Anand had parked the car. So he decided to use the brute force method to search. He took an elevator to the topmost floor and started to walk down, scanning cars parked on either side. He was down to the green level when he spotted his car. The car was parked towards the northern end of the green level, near a three foot high concrete barrier wall. As Sid approached the car he could see the expanse of the Symbiotic campus he had just traversed on bicycle. He was wondering how he would find Anand even if he had spotted the car, as this was not his usual time to leave. Surely the drivers didn't just hang out near their cars in this oppressive heat. Even though the parking deck was above ground and open from all sides, poor circulation heated up the stagnant air making the parking deck feel like an oven.

Sid was twenty feet away from the car when he spotted a tall figure wearing a jacket cross the campus courtyard from the auditorium towards the cafeteria building. Although the distance was far to get an accurate read, Sid was certain it was Scot Meyer crossing the courtyard. There were not that many tall people on the campus and hardly anyone who would wear a jacket in this heat. Sid's face hardened. He had to go back and accost Mr. Meyer. His behavior thus far had been very suspicious and Sid had to get to the bottom of it. *Was it perhaps a test that Brad Malone had designed for him? To evaluate how Sid dealt with such situations?* Sid sprinted to reach the edge of the parking deck to get a good view of the tall figure disappearing into the cafeteria building. Evidently Scot was in the auditorium just ten minutes ago when Sid called out to see if anyone was there. *Why didn't Scot reply then?*

Sid turned back and approached his car so he could keep his backpack in the car before going to the cafeteria. In the glare of the bright daylight he could just notice someone in the driver's seat slumped forward as if taking a nap. Sid tapped on the passenger side window to wake up Anand but there was no response. Sid knocked again, harder this time, yet there was no response. The glare didn't allow him a good view. So Sid walked around the back of the car towards the driver's window. What he saw was so horrible, he couldn't believe it. Sid gave out an involuntary scream that echoed through the parking deck. But no one was around and no one heard him.

Anand was slumped over the steering wheel, and a river of blood had left a bullet hole in his forehead and dried up along Anand's face. Dried blood covered the steering wheel too. Sid's jaw dropped. He was about to scream again for help, but quite obviously Anand was beyond needing any help. He must have been dead for a while.

He had to think fast. *What would Brad do under these circumstances?* Sid concluded this definitely wasn't a training exercise. Sid was sweating profusely, his heart beating fast. He pulled himself away from the car and rested his back on a concrete pillar nearby. He tried to yell for help but no sound came out of his parched throat.

CHAPTER 29

M itch Shelby was mad as hell and worried at the same time. He had just hung up the phone from a rather disturbing conversation with the CIA station chief for the Indian sub-continent. He had met Freddie Solomon personally a few times and had cultivated a good working relationship with Freddie when this whole affair of competitive advantage and industrial sabotage was emerging. Mitch was a shrewd CIA insider and knew the value of personal relationships.

In his previous meeting with Freddie, Mitch had shared the gist of the scrambled phone conversations his technician had spotted and recorded. Without giving his source, Mitch had conveyed just enough information to Freddie Solomon and had asked for his help to identify one of the voices. He wanted to know more information on the individual promising delivery of something important, a person who was deemed to be a Pakistani from Karachi.

As part of his responsibility, Freddie had cultivated and maintained many sources in India, Pakistan and Sri Lanka. After 9/11, the increased focus on Afghanistan had required him to further develop his network of informants inside Pakistan. During the subsequent years when the Iraq war became the front burner issue, Freddie had continued his efforts to penetrate the alphabet soup of terrorist organizations in Pakistan. It was his experience that the American dollar went a long way in obtaining whatever information he wanted. Besides, the various factions in Afghanistan and Pakistan were constantly in competition with each other, giving him many opportunities to dig out valuable information by simply using a divide, reward and conquer strategy.

Freddie's operatives were directly responsible for intercepting the chatter of impending attack on Mumbai. He had not personally met with David Headley as an informant, but with permission from the director, he was in touch with the F.B.I. agents who were secretly working with Mr. Headley. Again with permission from the director, he had shared the intelligence with the Indians only to watch the whole debacle of 26/11 unfold in front of him in Mumbai. Freddie had tried very hard to cultivate good relationship with the Indians, but he found it frustrating to deal with the bureaucracy and constant meddling of politicians. He had therefore developed a mistrust of the Indians when it came to operational matters such as execution on the ground. He often thought that no amount of intelligence gathering could help you if you could not muster the right boots on the ground to carry out missions.

What Freddie heard from Mitch Shelby gave him an independent corroboration of the chatter he was getting from his sources. Apparently, there was some insidious plot taking shape. According to his informants and analysts, a terrorist group was planning to strike at India's high technology establishments. The indications were not that of the 26/11 style attack causing horrible carnage which caused the whole world to sympathize with the Indians and cast a very long shadow on Pakistan. This was going to be something quite devastating in a different way and targeted a high technology operation. The thinking was to strike at what was becoming a crown jewel of India's progress.

The words shared by Mitch Shelby had lingered in Freddie's mind. *'Delivery of a package'* and *'traceable to our friends from East'* could mean a lot of different things, but Freddie was reaching a conclusion that frightened him. There wasn't enough information for him to make a classified report for the director as he had done in events leading to 26/11. But the analysis of what information he had, was leading to the location of Pune, a relatively smaller city on the Indian map, but an important one as far as both technology and military establishments were concerned.

Pune had always been a military base since before India's independence and the new sovereign India, after gaining independence from the British rule, had maintained and enhanced the military might in and around Pune. Freddie was aware of Sid Joshi's deployment in Pune and he knew that Sid was part of the computer security division headed by Mitch Shelby. Freddie had decided to call up Mitch to see if he could gain any further information that could illuminate some angles he had not thought about. In their previous face to face meetings, Freddie had liked and admired the plans Mitch had laid out and shared with Freddie. Mitch was obviously a very competent and agreeable individual. He would work with Mitch in the spirit of cooperation that the new director Pete Osborne had emphasized.

Their call lasted nearly fifteen minutes. Freddie had asked for the exact nature of Sid's mission and Mitch had shared the information. In return, Freddie shared what he knew.

A canister of material that could be used as a dirty nuclear bomb was missing in Pakistan. Apparently the material had come from North Korea to Pakistan and the canister bore coded information that could be traced to North Korea. There was a possibility that the same was in the hands of Al-Qaeda or some other terror group loosely affiliated with Al-Qaeda. And to top it all, the stolen material was headed for India and its likely destination was Pune.

Mitch sat motionless in his chair. He obviously didn't like what he heard. It wasn't his problem. His man was on the ground, but for an entirely different reason. Mitch hated missions that deviated from their purpose. His experience had told him how utterly messy things can get.

CHAPTER 30

Yusuf Gilani broke down in less than fifteen minutes.

General Chaudhry waited one day after he discovered the treachery of his orderly. He had to think through cautiously before pulling whichever trigger he had to pull. The first order of business was to find out who his orderly was working for. Was it the case of ISI internal rivalry or was it something else? He knew very well the dirty politics played within the ISI. It wasn't farfetched for some of the generals to plant a spy right under his nose. As a special advisor to the ISI chief, he was influential. His professional ways were not always appreciated by those bent more on ideology than military matters. Iqbal Chaudhry had survived all these years and had advanced because first and foremost he was a superb military strategist. And his loyalty to his country was above reproach. That didn't sit too well with some of the more radical factions within the ISI.

The second thing he must decide was the course of action to take based on who was controlling his orderly. If it was someone internal to ISI, he had already a plan in his mind. It will not be difficult to neutralize the adversary, whoever it was. But what if his orderly was bought over by the Americans or the Indians? What then?

General Chaudhry called his orderly to take him to the city. The general was dressed in inconspicuous civilian clothes suitable for physical activity. He wore a pair of khakis and a dark blue short sleeved shirt. As he dressed he watched himself in the mirror and flexed his triceps almost in an involuntary action. He was in good physical condition. Today he would have to use his strength to advantage. He wore hard soled leather shoes, a belt that could be used as a whip and slipped brass knuckles in his pocket. He had purchased the *coup de poing américain* during his student days in England when he made a few trips to France. He would do things the old fashioned way, *mano-a-mano*.

The car picked him up in front of the house.

"Where to sir?" asked his orderly.

"Just drive towards the river. I'll tell you where to go." The general replied.

There was a safe house near the river that General Chaudhry had used before. The house was in an upper middle class area where neighbors typically minded their own business. And the interrogation would be clean. That he knew for sure. He didn't believe in gory torture techniques. The General knew that his orderly owed him and had been loyal to him over the years, so breaking him based purely on personal level would be the best approach. He instructed his orderly to take several turns through a neighborhood and finally asked him to stop in front of an apartment building. General Chaudhry got out and motioned Yusuf to follow him.

They entered the building. Yusuf was surprised as he had never followed his master to any places of pleasure the General used to visit from time to time. He was somewhat excited in anticipation of seeing high society girls up close. They took steps to the fourth floor. The General took out keys from his pant pocket and unlocked the door of an apartment. He motioned Yusuf to follow him as he stepped inside.

But as soon as they entered, General Chaudhry shut the door behind him and held his orderly by the scruff of his neck. The general was good six inches taller than Yusuf and obviously far superior in terms of his social and military rank. Pakistani society is very class conscious and the elites are treated with deference. Yusuf was shocked to be held forcefully like that. His face clearly showed panic, confusion and utter disbelief.

General Chaudhry easily dragged him to a bedroom and sat him down in a chair the wrong way, facing the back of the chair. Yusuf was leaning forward clutching the backrest with his hands, his legs straddling the seat. His back was exposed. The General unbuckled and removed his belt swiftly in one motion. Before Yusuf could realize what was going to happen, the belt buckle came crashing down on the side of Yusuf's head, hard enough to cause a concussion without bleeding.

Yusuf was stunned by the violence. He looked into his masters eyes, which were filled with stone cold ruthless determination. No anger. Anger was a sign of weakness. The General was completely in command. Towering over Yusuf the general said in Urdu. *"Gaddari ki saza jaante ho?"*

It was a chilling question, reminding Yusuf of the penalty for treason.

Without waiting for an answer, a strong fist donning brass knuckles came crashing down on the left side of Yusuf's rib cage. He doubled over and would have collapsed from the vicious blow had it not been for the back of the chair supporting him. Yusuf's body went limp and his head fell forward.

"Kis ka namak khate ho?" Another rhetorical question followed by a blow of the belt buckle on the other side of Yusuf's head. This time reminding Yusuf that he owed his loyalty to the general.

General Chaudhry had moved to the back of Yusuf to lash out the belt in his right hand. Yusuf was close to losing consciousness. General Chaudhry kicked hard in Yusuf's lower back jarring his kidneys and making the chair fall down. Yusuf's face crashed on the marble floor and Yusuf started to bleed from his nose. General Chaudhry picked up Yusuf by his collar to a sitting position again.

Enough physical punishment for now, he thought to himself.

He dragged another chair in front of his orderly and sat down straddling his legs and keeping his folded hands on the back of the chair. He spoke in chillingly soothing tone. *"Muze khoon kharabi ka shauk nahin. Magar tum kuch bataoge nahin to haddi haddi todkar mar daloonga".*

The delivery was eerily convincing, warning Yusuf that the torture would continue if he didn't cooperate.

Yusuf had trouble speaking. He gasped for air. He was almost inaudible when he started to speak. Very slowly, bit by bit the information came out.

Yusuf's daughter had married Hamid, an ex-soldier who now was working for one of the militant organizations. Yusuf's cooperation was forced by threats of killing both his daughter and son-in-law. All he had to do was to eavesdrop on the General's conversation and report them word by word to Mohammed. He didn't know who Mohammed was or what his motives were. And this Mohammed was very happy when he heard the conversation between the Yankee and the General. Yusuf also blurted out the rendezvous details of his phone meetings with Mohammed.

General Chaudhry closed his eyes for a few seconds. He was thinking fast. The location where his orderly met this Mohammed and the fact that his son-in-law was working for this organization told him what he wanted to know. It was not a case of any foreign government spying on him. It was domestic trouble. *Or was it?* And then he thought of the delivery of the container. He had thought that delivery had gone well, as planned. And then suddenly it occurred to him.

The container most likely was delivered with the radioactive content, against his specific instructions to do otherwise. Why else would this extremist, this Mohammed, and the organization behind him go to such an extent to find out what was to transpire and then let it happen as the General had planned? It didn't make sense. And the Yankee had not protested when the General had changed his mind at the last minute, agreeing to deliver an empty container instead of a loaded one. In his mind, Iqubal Chaudhry was quickly assembling pieces of the puzzle.

With every second that went by he was more and more convinced that he had been outsmarted by someone. It just couldn't be explained in any other way. *Who was this Mohammed really working for? Was it the Americans? The Yankee he made the deal with?* It was reasonable to assume that the Yankee didn't like the last minute change of supplying an empty container. The Yankee had proven his resourcefulness in holding up his part of the deal, so he could have engineered a switch of orders. *Was a container with the radioactive material delivered instead of an empty one?* But then this Yankee didn't need a spy. He knew first hand that the General had decided to water down the delivery.

General Chaudhry was extremely worried. He didn't want to be the one to start an all out war between his country and the neighboring India. The outcome would be a total disaster for both of them. And how would the Indians react to finding a dirty bomb in one of their cities? An empty container, just a threat, would have been bad enough. He was sure that with intense diplomacy coupled with the obfuscation of North Korean traceability, the Indians could be calmed down. They always were looking for a reason not to take military action. The foreign investors in India would have been scared out of their wits bringing down or at least slowing down India's progress. But radioactive fallout was a totally different proposition. No government would sit idle. General Chaudhry was a patriot. He couldn't afford an all out war between the two countries. He must send a reconnaissance team to bring back the container. It had to be done at any cost.

General Chaudhry got up and put a glass of water in front of Yusuf.

"Clean up yourself and the floor." he said. "And don't bother to show me your face again." With those words General Chaudhry walked out of the apartment.

He had to act fast.

CHAPTER 31

S id was feeling utterly helpless. No training ever prepares one to deal with violent death at close quarters. Although he didn't know Anand that well, ever since coming to India in May, Sid had always depended on Anand to take him wherever he needed to go.

His mobile phone started to ring and gave Sid a start. He pulled the phone out of its carrying case and looked at it. His felt relieved. It was Sarah calling.

"Hi Sarah." the words barely came out of his mouth.

"Oh my gosh, are you alright?" Sarah's voice showed concern.

She could sense the tension in Sid's voice. There was silence at the other end. Sarah couldn't bear the silence although it was just a few seconds.

"Sid, how are you? Where are you? What's going on? You sound like you have sore throat. Have you seen a doctor?" The barrage of questions surged through the phone. Sid collected himself.

"Sarah I am so glad you called. Something terrible has happened. I have a favor to ask. Can you do something for me?" Sid whispered in the phone as he struggled to figure out a course of action.

"Of course Sid. What is it?" Sarah asked.

"Please contact Professor Levine immediately. I know it's late, but wake him up if you have to. My driver in India just got killed and I don't think it's a robbery gone awry or a gang war or anything like that." Sid had a chance to catch up his breath. He was thinking fast.

"It's something sinister. Something to do with the CIA mission. I am going to call Brad, my CIA contact. But something's just not right. Brad didn't tell me about any package to be delivered to Scot."

Sid's head was filled with simultaneous cross currents of various scenarios. All of a sudden his mind went back to the incident at his apartment. The smell lingering in his apartment and the hallway was remarkably similar to the scented tobacco that Anand usually chewed. Was Anand up to something? Was he working for someone else?

"Sid, please calm down. You aren't making any sense!" Sarah tried to reason with him. "Who is Scot? And are you in a safe place?" Sarah tried to be calm and reassuring.

Sid suddenly remembered watching Scot Meyer walking into the cafeteria building. He must get to Scot and find out what the hell was going on. He made up his mind and spoke in the phone as he started to walk to the stairs.

"Sarah, listen to me. Contact Professor Levine and tell him what I just told you. I am going to have a chat with Mr. Meyer. I won't call Brad until I know what was in my backpack."

With that he hung up and raced down the stairs.

Sarah sat motionless, holding the phone, looking shaken. She was across the world from Sid and he was in serious trouble. It was late even for her and calling Professor Levine at this hour felt awkward. But Sid had clearly told her otherwise. His words were fresh in her mind.

Please contact Professor Levine immediately. I know it's late, but wake him up if you have to.

Now it was Sarah's turn to feel helpless. She wished Sid had not hung up so abruptly. The panic in Sid's voice was so clear to her; she could feel it in her own body. Surely the CIA would do all they can to help Sid. They must. She decided to call the directory assistance number to get Professor Levine's number.

Sid climbed down the flight of stairs under thirty seconds. He darted out of the parking deck and almost ran to the security gate. He touched his security card on to the pole reader and rushed through the gate. He removed a community bicycle from its stand and sped towards the cafeteria. It took him barely a minute to cross the distance. He left the bicycle at a stand and walked quickly into the cafeteria. As he entered, he realized he was attracting attention. He moved his fingers through his hair, patting it down, brought a smile to his face and picked up a tray. He picked up a sandwich, walked through the checkout line paying the cashier and emerged into the huge dining hall. It wasn't hard to spot Scot sitting by the glass wall directly in front of him.

Sid tried to walk casually through a maze of tables and chairs towards Scot and put his tray on the table.

"Can I join you?" Sid flashed a smile to mask the state of his mind. Without waiting for a reply, Sid sat down across from Scot.

"Scot I am so sorry, I totally forgot I was carrying the parcel for you." Sid tried to project a friendly tone, but it was hard. "You know how it is. I have been working on sealing a loophole in the flash ROM code. I sort of forget everything else when I have a problem to solve."

Sid smiled and looked to Scot for a response. "Hope everything worked out for you." Sid added to elicit a response.

Scot was sort of relieved. In typical spy games one spy didn't know what the other was told. But it was inconceivable that Sid would carry such a package and not know about it. Scot smiled in return.

"Hey, no problem. You're a good bloke. I know you guys just get lost in your work. That's so fantastic."

Sid looked at his sandwich. He had no desire to eat. He had to figure out where the parcel was. He had inadvertently carried something in his backpack this morning, but he had no idea what it was. He must figure out what it might contain. The events unfolded thus far told him that the parcel must be something sinister if people were ready to kill for it or for the parcel to reach where they intended it to reach. With great effort, Sid tried to be sly and with a fake smile he lowered his voice to a conspiratorial tone.

"So where did you leave it in the auditorium?" Sid asked.

His heart was thumping loudly giving a throbbing sound in his temples. But Scot didn't seem to notice it. He replied casually. "It's under a seat in the second row towards the center of the auditorium. I'll set the timer in another hour or so. Then we've got seventy two hours."

The words caused a searing pain in Sid's chest. *Set the timer? Then we've got seventy two hours? What in the hell was this parcel? Was it a bomb?*

Scot seemed to be unaware of Sid's state of mind. Scot continued. "But it'll be discovered before that in day after tomorrow's event. So the panic will hit high pitch by noon that day. I, for one don't plan to be around. What's your plan?"

Sid mumbled something and coughed to hide his emotions. He was having difficulty even breathing normally.

"You alright man?" Scot called out. There was no response from Sid. Sid gave a weak smile and excused himself as he got up from the table. Scot shrugged his shoulders and continued to eat his chicken curry.

Sid knew what he had to do.

CHAPTER 32

Roger Patel was not happy paying the fat fee to Arnold & Gregg on top of that exorbitant sum to the mysterious man. Their consulting fee rates were expensive. And the other payment was surely destined to a slush fund controlled by the party he had talked to. But then again, Arnold & Gregg was the best in what they did. And what was the alternative? Lose control of his business? The business he had started from nothing and had worked so hard to grow to this point? To make it worse, he had to pay the large sum from his own pocket. Fiduciaries in his company would have never approved a payout of this magnitude to the lobbying firm that acted as a conduit.

And what was he getting in return? A vague, conspiratorial promise. A promise of trying to disrupt the business of his main rival, the eight hundred pound gorilla in the embedded chip business. No, his board or anybody else in his company must never find out about this payout. And most importantly, they must never find out what he was supposed to get in return.

Of course the official story for this transaction, even though there were no receipts given or book entries made, was supposed to be that it was for consulting services with respect to the bill H.R. 19623. Even though the fee was way out of a normal range, one could explain it away. And if everything went according to plans, he was told, the payback to Pinnacle Systems would be a windfall, restoring its financial health. All the inconvenient nagging and threats from his board of directors would simply go away. Nobody questions a strong balance sheet and nobody would ask questions about the miraculous recovery of his company.

But the businessman in him was asking tough questions. What were the plans? What would this influential friend of Jim Arnold do to make Symbiotic Research Labs take a dive? What was his motive? Surely he had paid a lot of money, but Roger was convinced there was something more than money driving this individual. The edge in this person's voice during the uncomfortable conversation at Jim Arnold's office had told Roger that this individual was motivated more by ideology than money. But what sort of ideology makes you disrupt someone's business? Surely what was going to transpire couldn't be legal.

Roger felt tightness in his chest. Was he going too far? Even though the lobbying firm had given him deniability as he didn't know the modus operandi or the exact effect of what was promised in secrecy. If anyone raised questions, Roger could simply deny any complicity in whatever was going to happen.

And then there were his personal feelings. His conscience was troubling him ever since that meeting at Arnold & Gregg. Illegal or not, what he was doing was certainly not ethical. Over the years there had been times when he had crossed the line. But he was always able to rationalize his actions simply as business practice, arguing that if he didn't do it, someone else would. Such logic had been routinely applied by countless business people all over the world.

This time however, it was different for Roger. No doubt the stakes were high. His survival as an influential businessman was on the line. His business was at the core of who he was. Was he ready to accept defeat in life by losing control of his company? There were no easy answers, although the right answer was to do the right thing and unwind the gears of this conspiracy before it hurt innocent people who were certain to lose their livelihood.

Roger was suddenly feeling sick in his stomach. His closest friend, his only friend, was his dad who had passed away a few years earlier. Roger was divorced a long time ago after just a couple of years of married life. He had no time for a wife. And in his business dealings he held all the cards close to his chest. He had not bothered to groom a successor. Roger felt utterly lonely as he sat in his huge office.

On impulse, Roger picked up the phone. He wanted to confront Jim Arnold, but Roger was smart enough to realize that he didn't have a strong hand in dealing with Jim. So he decided to contact Todd Lester. Roger didn't have Todd's direct number, so he called the Arnold & Gregg main line.

"Todd Lester please. This is Roger Patel of Pinnacle Systems." he said to the operator.

"Just a moment please." was the polite reply.

The operator had typed the word 'Pinnacle' on her computer screen and her screen popped up a 'not found' message. She tried again with fewer letters making sure she was entering it properly. But she received the same message.

Then she looked up Todd Lester. He was shown as a senior associate of the firm. The operator was puzzled, but chalked up this as possibly a cold call from a potential client. Her instructions were clear. She was supposed to hand over the call to one of the junior associates.

"Excuse me sir, Mr. Lester is not available at the moment. I will transfer you to Ms. Debbie Elliott who will help you."

Roger was puzzled and irritated. He had called the main number at Arnold & Gregg before, and the operator had always put him through. Roger knew the basics of the Customer Relationship Management systems. After all, his company, Pinnacle Systems had one of the world's largest CRM practice.

"This is Debbie Elliott. Sorry for the wait Mr. Patel. How can I be of help?" The junior associate was courteous.

And the irritation in Roger's voice was obvious as he spoke.

"I need to speak with Todd Lester. My company Pinnacle Systems is a client of yours. I sign large checks to your firm. Now please find Mr. Lester for me and put him on." Roger said curtly.

Debbie Elliott was confused. There was no record of Pinnacle Systems or Roger Patel in the firm's database. But something in Roger's voice convinced her to find Todd.

"Sir, I apologize again. Please hold and I will try to locate Mr. Lester for you."

Roger was not used to holding a phone line for someone to answer him. So by the time Todd Lester answered, he was quite angry.

"Hello Mr. Patel, this is Todd Lester. I am sorry for the glitch. How are you?"

"I have been better." Replied Roger icily. "I have some questions. I just want to better understand this arrangement we discussed in your office."

"Certainly, perhaps I can have Jim Arnold call you?" Todd said politely.

"That won't be necessary. I would rather discuss it with you. You were there when we had the call with Jim's contact who spoke with us. What's his name?" asked Roger casually.

Todd was taken aback for two reasons. First, the Pinnacle Systems and Roger Patel were missing from the firm's client database. As if they didn't exist. As if they never had a conversation. This was unusual. Secondly, it was made very clear to Roger during that rather awkward meeting that the other party wished to stay anonymous. Roger had initially objected, but after listening to persuasive arguments from Jim and the other party, he had agreed to the terms.

So why was Roger so curious now?

They talked for ten minutes or so. Todd danced around the main issue, using verbal gymnastics to placate Roger. It was one of the most uncomfortable conversations Todd remembered. This notion of causing disruptions in a competitor's operations was perhaps illegal. He didn't know the laws of the land and how it was all going down. But it was certainly unethical. Squeezing a competitor in trade negotiations was one thing. Promising to cause problems so they lost market share was something else entirely.

Roger was not satisfied, but Todd promised to find Jim and get answers for Roger.

He made a note to ask Jim why he would want to erase Roger's record as a client. *What scheme was Jim cooking up here? Was*

Oliver Martin receiving funds or was Jim keeping the entire sizable fee? What exactly was Oliver going to do to deliver what he had promised?

As usual there were more questions than answers. He had to think hard about whether he wanted to continue working at the firm.

CHAPTER 33

Sid entered his office building, climbed the stairs to his floor and walked to his cubicle. Using his computer, he logged into his company email account. He made an entry indicating he would be out of office for couple of days as he wasn't feeling well. He then turned off the laptop and put it in his backpack. He turned off the work lights and left his cubicle. Sid walked back all the way to the end of the building on his floor where emergency exit stairs were. He didn't want to take a chance of bumping into anyone he knew, especially Scot Meyer. Sid took steps all the way to the ground floor and emerged from the building using a side exit. He then proceeded directly to the auditorium keeping normal pace although he wanted to sprint there.

The auditorium was unused on most days. With a capacity of one thousand, it was a popular venue for large company events. Symbiotic Research Labs was known to be an employee friendly place. Employees were encouraged to gather for recreational activities ranging from rock bands to meditation camps. Any registered employee group could book the auditorium by requesting it from the cultural director. The fusion jazz group had invited a well known Indian percussion player to perform in a couple of days. All events were always free and open to all employees. This particular event was expected to draw a large crowd, almost filling the auditorium.

Sid walked through the lobby, retracing his steps from his earlier visit today. The auditorium was dark. Some light was filtering in from couple of open doors on each side. The maintenance staff usually kept these doors open to allow adequate air circulation. Sid walked down the sloping floor towards the front of the auditorium. He squinted to get a better view of the rows of seats towards the front of the auditorium. He turned right from the center isle into the second row of seats. He raised each seat and looked closely if anything was under it. He covered the distance of ten seats but didn't see anything tucked under the seats. He then turned back and started searching under the seats on the left side of the isle. He found a brown paper bag below the third seat. He looked inside the bag. There was a cylindrical object not unlike a capsule used at a bank drive through. The cylinder however was much heavier and metallic. There was a keypad and a small digital display at one end of the cylinder. It wasn't anything Sid had ever seen before. But the keypad and the digital display reminded him of what Scot had said about *setting it* after lunch.

Sid picked it up and carried it to the side of the auditorium towards one of the open doors. He examined it in the daylight. There were color coded markings on the cylindrical surface, akin to a bar code. And there were some symbols he couldn't recognize. Sid was puzzled. *What could it be?* The weight was certainly consistent with the weight of his backpack this morning. Sid remembered how the backpack straps were digging into his shoulders.

Scot's words were echoing in Sid's ears. *I will set the timer in an hour or so* he had said.

Was this a bomb? Why would Scot set off a bomb if he worked for the CIA or some affiliate? Nothing made any sense. Sid put the cylinder in his backpack, zipped it close and entered the lobby carrying the backpack on his right shoulder. Just then his phone rang. Sid pressed the talk button.

"Hello Sid, this is Mitch Shelby." the voice said.

Sid didn't recognize the voice nor did the name ring any bells.

"I am sorry, who did you say you are?" Sid asked.

"I am a friend of Dr. Richard Levine and the boss of Brad Malone." the voice continued.

Sid suddenly remembered the name and connected it to a face he had come across during his introductions the first week at Langley.

"Oh, good afternoon Mr. Shelby, or good morning I guess depending on where you are." Sid replied.

"Thanks Sid." Mitch Shelby continued. "We have reasons to believe that you may have gotten drawn into things that were not of your concern." Mitch wanted to put Sid's mind at ease. "Someone has broken into your apartment and may be using you to smuggle in something to the Symbiotic Research Labs premises. We have reasons to believe that it may be your driver in India." Now Mitch was speaking in a tone that had an edge to it.

By this time, Sid was frazzled beyond limit. He wasn't entirely sure whom he could trust. Anand's dead body would be discovered soon. Would he be in big trouble?

"Sid, do not panic or do something stupid. Do not call the local authorities and do not call Brad Malone. You must wait for further instructions from us, from me."

Sid was flabbergasted. The deputy director of his division had called him out of the blue and knew of the unusual happenings of the day. Sid was feeling uneasily suspicious.

"I am sorry sir, but how do I know it's you?" Sid had to ask.

Mitch was expecting to be challenged. In fact he would have been very disappointed if he was not. *This guy has presence of mind,* Mitch thought. He continued to speak.

"Sid, you may not trust me as we have never met and you don't know me. Therefore I have someone here on the line you do know. Richard you there?"

"Yes I am here Mitch." Sid was relieved to hear the familiar voice of his mentor and teacher, Professor Richard Levine.

"Hello Dr. Levine. I am so glad you are here. In fact I had asked Sarah to contact you."

Sid felt like a pressure valve had released the tension in his mind. It would be comforting to share the bizarre happenings of the day with someone he trusted.

"Sid, I know. Sarah did contact me and she told me everything. How are you holding up?" Professor Levine asked and proceeded to explain further.

"I called Mr. Shelby as he is the right guy to instruct you on what you need to do. And I am so sorry that things have turned rather ugly. But bear with us and do exactly what Mitch here tells you. Are you okay with that?"

"I guess." Sid replied.

"Then I am going to drop off now, so you two can discuss what you need to do. Okay? And good luck."

With that Professor Levine disconnected from the conversation.

"Sid, are you still there?" Mitch Shelby's voice continued.

"Yes, I am here. And I have just located whatever this person Scot Meyer had brought to the auditorium."

Sid wanted to get everything off his chest. But Mitch Shelby stopped him.

"Sid, wait. Are you in a place where you can talk without being overheard? If not, find a private place, walk there and don't hang up. I will hold."

Sid scanned the lobby. There wasn't a soul around. But even the slightest sound was reverberating through the empty lobby. He looked around and found stairs leading to the greenrooms behind the auditorium stage. Sid took the short flight of stairs and entered one of the small dressing rooms. He closed the door behind him and locked it.

"Hello?" he talked into the phone to make sure he still had a good signal.

"Yes Sid, I am here. Now tell me everything from the beginning. Don't leave out anything, however inconsequential it may sound."

"Sure."

Sid answered and started narrating everything he could think of.

Mitch stopped Sid from time to time to ask him to clarify some points. He asked Sid to tell him Scot's full name and spelling so he could search in various databases, perhaps contact the MI6. The conversation continued for the next fifteen minutes. Sid was feeling relieved to get it all off his chest to someone who could do something about it. After listening to Sid's narration, Mitch started giving instructions.

"Let me tell you son, you have done well." Mitch said in a compassionate tone.

"Now listen to me carefully. Do not call anyone, not even Brad. Do not call the local authorities. We'll take care of that. I want you to leave the Symbiotic campus immediately."

More instructions kept flowing over the phone.

"Take with you the object you just found and your laptop. Do not show it to anybody. Go find a secluded, open place where no one is around and then call me at the number I am going to tell you."

Mitch waited a few seconds to give Sid a chance to absorb everything. Then he continued.

"Sid, make sure the place where you go is in the open. No trees or buildings nearby for at least ninety square feet of land. And memorize the number I am going to tell you. Do not write it down anywhere."

Mitch said and paused. "Can you do it all in the next half-hour? You must do it in the next half hour. I am counting on you."

Sid looked at his watch. It was almost forty five minutes past four in the afternoon.

"Yes Mr. Shelby. Half-hour is difficult, but I am sure I can do it in the next forty-five minutes." Sid replied.

"Very well then. Here is the number I want you to remember." Then Mitch gave Sid his private number. He wanted to confirm again that Sid had understood the time limit.

"You must do this in the next forty-five minutes, before it gets dark. Can you?"

"Yes Mr. Shelby. I can." Sid replied.

He was surprised to hear the confidence in his own voice.

CHAPTER 34

Pune is situated at the northwestern edge of India's Deccan Plateau. It's nestled among rolling hills on three sides except the east. These are the hills that lead to the Sahyadri mountain range. Immediately to west of the city are chains of smaller hills that form a network of trails frequented by hiking enthusiasts.

Many locations among these hills are well known for their historic significance. Some of the freedom fighters, trying to overthrow the British rule in India, had collaborated and plotted against the British in the very same hills. And going further back in history to the eighteenth century, the favorite hero of the region, King Shivaji had fought the Mughal aggression in the very same mountains and hills of Maharashtra, denying the Mughal King Aurangzeb a clean sweep of the Deccan.

Sid had found out about these trails from some of his co-workers. He had routinely embarked on exploration of the hiking trails on weekends. He preferred to climb alone as he could keep a steady pace and cover more ground. Apart from visiting the fitness center he belonged to, the weekend hikes in these parts was Sid's favorite physical activity to stay fit as well as to dodge terrible pollution that engulfed the city.

Sid was thinking about what Mitch Shelby had said. *Find a secluded, open space and take your laptop with you.* He obviously meant the laptop issued by his unit in the CIA. Sid always carried his CIA laptop in his car, but couldn't bring it on the Symbiotic campus due to security rules of the company. The thought of going back to his car was unnerving. The sight of Anand's slumped body was still fresh in his mind. And he knew that soon the body would be discovered as other drivers start returning to their vehicles to pick up their rides.

It was almost five p.m. local time. He had less than two hours of daylight and he needed to hurry. He was also worried about his own physical safety. Whatever was in the cylindrical package that he was carrying was obviously an instrument of destruction of some sort. It was reassuring to hear from Scot that the device needed to be armed with a timer to set it off and the fact that Scot had still not done so. But even then, carrying the device on his person made Sid quite nervous. Whatever this thing was, it was evidently of high importance to someone. *Important enough to kill.*

That was another piece of this evolving puzzle Sid couldn't fathom.

Who killed Anand and why? What was Anand's role in all this?

Mitch Shelby had said that he suspected Anand of planting the device into Sid's backpack. *But how? And when?*

Then suddenly Sid recollected the events of the morning. His car was relatively new and in good condition. He thought it was strange that his car had some mechanical problem on his way to work. He didn't think much of it at that time as he was thinking of Sarah and had called her while waiting for the repair work. But now that he thought of it he remembered some onlookers gather around his car that morning when Anand was trying to fix it. It wasn't uncommon in India to attract idle onlookers for anything, *but did one of them plant the device? Or were they working with Anand to give him cover of confusion so Sid wouldn't notice anything?*

On many occasions, Brad had given him several pearls of wisdom. Things that an agent must know.

"Always trust your instincts and most importantly, be tuned in to what your instincts tell you."

Sid could hear in his mind Brad's voice and could imagine his stern face.

"Whether you are in social situations in company of people or alone, you must always be sensitive to your surroundings. Pick up on anything unusual, however trivial it may seem to you."

Sid cursed himself. He had let down his guard this morning. As he thought about it more, Sid was convinced that Anand must have put the device in his backpack right then, as he was ostensibly repairing the broken vehicle. But it was too late for self-criticism. He had limited time to act.

Sid's immediate problem was how to get away from the Symbiotic campus. He couldn't drive the car with a dead body at the wheel. Asking someone for a ride was out of the question. But first he must retrieve his laptop from the trunk of the car.

Sid came out of the greenroom and entered the auditorium lobby. The lobby was still deserted. He quietly exited the auditorium and walked towards the bicycle he had used to get there. As he mounted the bicycle, he noticed a group of employees walking towards the auditorium entrance. Sid turned and pushed hard on pedals going uphill in the other direction. He gathered enough speed to propel himself over the lawn and the curb towards a gulley downhill that led to the street in a roundabout fashion. He thought of his childhood days when riding bicycle through neighborhood yards and streams and cutting through parking lots was a routine. Now it made him self-conscious but he had no choice. He eventually circled around to the main road and pushed hard on pedals to reach the security gate.

Again, he left the community bicycle at the stand. Surely the security alarm would go off with what he was carrying, just as it had in the morning on his way in. Sid didn't want to take a chance. He didn't go through the security gate, but instead headed for the security office. He made a complaint that his access card was faulty and needed a new one. He also explained that he was in hurry and would stop by tomorrow.

He then came out and walked around the security gate. No one suspected anything. Sid counted his blessings and walked towards the parking deck.

Sid quickly climbed the four sets of stairs in the parking deck to reach the Green level. He was breathing hard from pedaling his bicycle and sprinting up the stairs. He walked to his car, and without looking at Anand, he unlocked and opened the trunk with the duplicate keys he had tucked away in his backpack and picked up his CIA issue laptop. As he moved away from the car a plan started to formulate in his head.

He quickly took stairs to reach the two-wheeler parking level and entered the large area where thousands of scooters and motorcycles were parked. Surely he would find here what he was looking for. Sid had always been a motorcycle buff. He had worked on his used Ducati extensively in Birmingham. In Pune he owned a Bajaj Avenger motorcycle and rode it for fun on weekends and evenings. Navigating around the narrow and crowded streets of Pune was far easier on a two-wheeler than a car.

Sid scanned the rows of motorcycles until he found a Bajaj Avenger. He tested to see if the handlebar was locked in place; it was. Sid continued to move, looking for the same make until he found one that had its handlebar unlocked. He put his backpack in the carrying case on the left side of the motorcycle. To bypass the ignition key mechanism was an easy task. He mounted the motorcycle and pulled the wires going into the ignition switch. He tried to short the two open ends of the wire by his right hand.

"Damn it!" he exclaimed in frustration as the wires slipped from his fingers.

The wires were short and hard to manage by one hand. He could barely get his fingers on them. Sid tried again several times using both hands until the wire ends touched each other. He then twisted them together to keep the wires locked.

With a sigh of relief Sid pushed the motorcycle backwards. Once out of its parking space, Sid kicked the starting pedal, bringing the motorcycle engine to life. There was no helmet, so he would have to ride without one. It was illegal in Pune to ride without a helmet, but then again, it was also illegal to steal a motorcycle. Nonetheless, he picked up an unlocked helmet from one of the motorcycles around and tried it on. It fit him well. Sid was relieved.

Sid accelerated out of the parking deck, going uphill towards the road leading to the highway. A silver colored Tavera SUV was parked outside the parking deck. As soon as Sid sped by, the two occupants of the car looked at each other in panic, and started the car. The SUV merged onto the road, keeping a distance of a hundred meters behind Sid.

On a nearby hill two men had been waiting by a parked car, taking turns to keep a watch using binoculars. The man who was watching the silver Tavera said something to the other man in Urdu. They talked to each other animatedly for a few seconds and jumped into the parked car. The car screeched as it lurched forward and started to accelerate downhill on a dirt road.

Within a minute the car swung onto the road following the silver Tavera at a safe distance. The man in the passenger seat pulled out an automatic gun tucked in waistline of his pants and checked it. The ease with which he handled the gun indicated his expertise with the weapon. The driver spoke out in Urdu.

"You stupid, keep that away. We are only supposed to watch the CIA and grab the package if they or their man has it." The driver was obviously in command. He drove silently for a minute and then added another rebuke. "Don't you do anything stupid. We got to play this safe and from distance, unless of course we can't. But let me be the judge of that."

The driver's name was Hafez. He was from a close-knit elite spy unit of Pakistan. General Chaudhry had personally recruited him and had been his mentor over the last ten years. And the General's orders were very clear. No violence unless provoked. And to get the container from the Symbiotic campus or from wherever it would be. Hafez had been activated only a few hours back and had flown to Pune from New Delhi where he lived. He had hooked up with a local man in Pune who did a lot of work for the Pakistanis.

Hafez had no idea how he could break into the Symbiotic campus and look for something smaller than a duffel bag. He had asked his local contact to drive him in the general area where Symbiotic

Research Labs was located. His idea was to scout the terrain, looking for weak spots to enter at night. He was just passing the main entrance to Symbiotic Labs when he came across a silver Tavera and recognized the face of the driver. Hafez had known that man to be a mercenary, connected to a local gang. It was well known in the gang circle that the man often worked for the Americans.

What is he doing here? Hafez thought. Then it hit him. *This man was perhaps after the same thing that Hafez himself was looking for?*

Hafez decided to hide and observe what the driver in the silver Tavera was up to. He would follow him to figure out if he was going to break in the campus. That would make his job easy. He could simply grab the container from the man and run from Pune.

He must not lose tail of that silver Tavera. And whoever was riding the motorcycle like a mad man was obviously in possession of the package that both he and the Americans were looking for.

CHAPTER 35

M itch Shelby was in the waiting area of the director's office. He had decided to escalate the matter to the director, Pete Osborne. Loose nuclear material was always a top concern and the director had agreed to see Mitch right away. Mitch had briefly talked about the urgency of the matter and the fact that all this was taking place in a friendly country without the knowledge of the local authorities.

Mitch needed to see the director rather urgently for several reasons. First and foremost he had to verify with some certainty that the package Sid was carrying was indeed a dirty nuclear bomb. To do that without alerting the Indians was going to be tricky. The secret conversations he had listened to were now leading him to believe that some rogue elements in Pakistan were involved. This was also corroborated by the CIA station chief based in India, Freddie Solomon. Mitch was also aware that the rogue elements within CIA and the Pentagon, who had hijacked his mission, probably had their people watching and would not hesitate to intervene, perhaps causing harm to his agent and jeopardizing his mission. Any missteps could cause havoc and a chain reaction of international tit-for-tat, which could easily escalate into a full-fledged war. Mitch certainly didn't want to be responsible for that.

"The director will see you now." the director's executive assistant informed him.

Mitch got up and followed her to the office of Pete Osborne, the CIA director.

Mr. Osborne motioned Mitch to sit down in a chair at his rather expansive desk. A lot of sensitive, top secret information was routinely discussed around this desk.

If only the desk had ears, Mitch thought to himself. The director put down a file he was looking at.

"Well Mitch tell me what's all this about. What in God's name are we doing with loose nuclear material in India?"

Pete Osborne was known to be astute, direct, and fair. Mitch was getting a firsthand experience of one of these three qualities of the director. Mitch cleared his throat and decided to reciprocate the directness of his boss.

"Mr. Director, I have an agent placed in India to gather profiles of some of the scientists working on the next generation of chips used in embedded systems." Mitch started to explain. "I have reasons to believe that an unauthorized mission has been undertaken by someone in the CIA or in the Pentagon to plant a dirty nuclear bomb at the location where my agent is and they have used him to unwittingly plant the bomb."

Mitch paused to swallow and let the director Osborne digest the news. He then continued. "As of right now, my man has the bomb package in his possession and I need to use our satellites to unobtrusively verify that the package he is carrying is indeed what we think it is, and also to understand its mechanics and how it may be diffused."

Director Osborne motioned with his hand to stop Mitch.

"Hold on Mitch. What's this embedded systems business? I do remember hearing about it from someone. And what's the connection to a dirty nuclear bomb?"

Mitch did not want to digress. But he was obliged to give a brief summary of the whole embeddable systems threat initiative. He hurried through the explanation and came back to his original point.

"Mr. Director, if what I suspect about this dirty nuclear bomb is true, we need to handle the situation very delicately and get the bomb away from India."

Pete Osborne let out a sigh. He removed his reading glasses and looked straight at Mitch. His tone was dead serious as he spoke. "These are serious allegations Mr. Shelby. I hope you are wrong. We have learnt a thing or two since the Iran Contra affair. Have we not?"

Mitch was about to protest. But Director Osborne continued. "However we can't take a chance that you may be right, and by golly if you are right about this, we have to stop this mess right now."

Mitch sat back, sensing the conversation was going in the right direction. The director continued. "We can't take a chance of unrest in the Indian sub-continent when we are fighting this war on terror on multiple fronts."

Mitch was relieved to see that director was getting engaged. His worst fear was that the director may just rebuff him as spinning something not plausible.

"What do you need to verify the precise nature of this dirty bomb, if that's what it is?"

Mitch was hoping to hear this. "Mr. Director, I need to enlist help from our nuclear scientists in Los Alamos, who are watching the proliferation of loose nuclear material, especially from North Korea." Mitch said.

The reference of North Korea caused real discomfort to the director as evidenced by several wrinkles that appeared on his forehead. Pete Osborne got up from his chair and started moving around as if to lessen the tension in his body. Mitch continued. "We believe that some of the spent nuclear material from North Korea found its way to Pakistan and now is in the hands of my agent. We need the use of our military covert satellites with highest resolution to take pictures of this container and quickly evaluate what it is. Then I need . . ."

Director Osborne stopped Mitch by raising his hand. "Let's not get ahead of ourselves Mitch. You got what it takes to do the verification."

The director stopped pacing and rested against the edge of his desk, looking Mitch in the eye. "Keep me posted as soon as you know something. I will have to alert the President if this container is in fact a dirty bomb. We'll plan the next steps once we know for sure."

Mitch knew the meeting was over. But he had a go ahead for what he was hoping to put in place.

CHAPTER 36

Sid rumbled down the road connecting Symbiotic campus to the highway. The road was wide and paved to smooth perfection for the first two kilometers and then deteriorated quickly where ownership of the campus developer ended. Beyond that, local authorities did not maintain the road in good condition despite the tax windfall they had benefitted from since large multi-national companies had set up operations there.

The potholes and uneven, narrow pavement made it a challenge to drive. On top of that, the unruly and ubiquitous auto rickshaws, the staple transport of many Indian cities, made it impossible to drive at the posted speed limits. Pedestrians and hawkers pedaling their merchandise always outnumbered vehicles and acted as if they owned the road. In the chaotic traffic of Pune, a two-wheeler had an upper hand over larger cars. Sid's pursuers were discovering this reality in trying to keep up with their subject.

In the silver Tavera was a pair of operatives for hire. They often did contract work for the CIA and the MI6, ranging from minor tasks that required intimate knowledge of the city to contract killings. They sometimes undertook strong arm tactics on behalf of credit card companies and other private debt collectors. This time their instructions were to keep an eye on one Sid Joshi after taking care of his driver. Since the job was done, they had no use for Anand and their instructions were to not leave any loose ends. They had tailed Sid for some time now and knew him well enough to recognize him and his car. The people who had hired them were supposed to call as their subject exited the Symbiotic campus that day. They were supposed to just follow him and send an alert if Sid Joshi behaved in an unusual way. Their clients must have tapped into the company's security system, looking for the record of Sid passing through the front security gate. They were told to be ready a while back but no one had come out of the parking deck. Besides how could this Sid use his car? There was a dead body at the steering wheel.

That's why they were surprised when without any warning a speeding motorcycle darted out of the parking deck. The operatives in Tavera were sure it was Sid and they had started to follow him. This of course was highly unusual behavior and they would call in just as soon as this Sid guy stopped somewhere. But the way he was riding, like a maniac, it was proving to be difficult to keep up with him. The chase was on.

Unknown to the CIA hired goons; the ISI operatives were following them in a beat up Ford at a safe distance. Their idea was to tail the CIA operatives who presumably were following someone who had the bomb or was involved in some way.

The driver of the Tavera cursed in Marathi, the local language spoken in Pune, as he swerved to avoid a pedestrian. "*Tichya mayala, rasta kay tuzya bapa cha ahe kay?*"

He was having a difficult time keeping up with the motorcycle which was easily navigating the crowded road. He aggressively pushed forward his vehicle on the wrong side of the road trying to pass a clutter of rickshaws. His action caused a cacophony of shrill horns from the cars going in the opposite direction. One of those cars swerved to the left to avoid the oncoming Tavera and ended up hitting another car, starting a chain reaction of collisions. The resulting noise caught Sid's attention as he looked in his right side mirror. He noticed the Tavera accelerating towards him. It looked familiar and Sid immediately realized it was the same SUV he had noticed just outside the Symbiotic parking deck. Someone was following him. It wasn't entirely unexpected. He had to get rid of the tail well before reaching the spot where he was going.

Sid was approaching the highway overpass. He prayed for a green traffic light so he wouldn't have to wait to turn right, going towards the highway onramp. His prayers were heard and answered. The signal had just turned green. Sid joined the unruly caravan of vehicles ranging from large buses to man-pulled carts used for goods transportation over short distances. Although highway didn't allow non-motorized vehicles, the road going straight through the traffic light was a surface road, and nobody followed the discipline of leaving the rightmost lanes to the traffic merging onto the highway. Sid took a sharp right turn careening his motorcycle as the Tavera and the Ford pushed their way through the intersection about two hundred meters behind.

The pursuit was on. Sid wasn't trained to evade threatening pursuers. But he had to get out of this situation.

Sid accelerated his motorcycle and merged into the already thickening traffic on the highway going towards the city. He passed several slow moving cars and trucks, weaving his way at ease. Anywhere else it would have been a suicidal maneuver, but not in India, and especially not in Pune. The large crop of young, brash IT workers that had descended on the city from all over India were known to ride motorcycles as if they were playing a video game.

After riding ten minutes like a possessed man, Sid scanned his mirrors to look for the Tavera that was following him. It was nowhere in sight, but Sid didn't want to take a chance. He got off the highway two exits before where he wanted to get off. He would ride on small surface streets where anybody following him would be more obvious. Sid wasn't sure if there were any other cars or even motorcycles tailing him. He turned abruptly into the grassy patch to the left of the highway, revved up his motorcycle as he came up a shallow ditch in his way onto a small road running parallel to the highway. He turned left going in the opposite direction and scanned the open expanse of grass to see if any other vehicle followed him. He didn't see anyone.

Sid reduced his speed to avoid an accident on the surface street. He could hear his heart beating. His shirt was drenched with sweat and there were rivers of sweat flowing from his temples. The Pune heat, although dry, was not forgiving. But Sid had no time to waste. He had promised Mitch Shelby that in forty five minutes he would be at a safe, secluded location that afforded a clear view from the sky. Instinctively Sid glanced up towards the sky. There would be daylight for another forty five minutes or so.

CHAPTER 37

PUNE, INDIA:

Pune offers its citizens some unique hiking spots right in the middle of the busy city. Many of these spots have historic significance due to the rich history of freedom fighters, both against the Mughal Empire and later in the British rule over India. The undulating landscape of Pune is dotted with small hills and trails connecting them. What precious little green, open spaces that are left in Pune can be attributed to the presence of large defense establishments and these hiking trails. One of these hiking spots is the *Vetal Tekdi*.

A literal translation of *Vetal Tekdi* does not make sense. Among myriads of Hindu gods is a deity called *Vetal*, which roughly means a ghost of some powers or a demon god. There have always been sects among Hindus who have secretly worshipped gods that most common people would not. It is said that the deity of *Vetal* expects blood sacrifice to keep him at bay so as not to bother ordinary people.

Vetal is also considered to be beneficial protector of cemeteries and remote places. *Tekdi* in Marathi language means a hill. So appropriately enough, the *Vetal Tekdi* is a hill dotted by a small, almost unnoticeable temple of *Vetal*. Even today, some people go and visit the temple and sometimes sacrifice a chicken or a goat, but for most Puneites, it's a place for hiking and getting a breath of fresh air.

For Sid, it had been both a place for hiking and a place of solitude. One thing that bothered him in Pune was that there were no places within easy reach where one was alone. Sid had hooked up with some co-workers who frequented many of the hiking spots on weekends. After a few group hikes, Sid started to hike on his own. The *Vetal Tekdi* was the closest spot from his apartment.

LANGLEY, VIRGINIA:

While Sid was negotiating the highway traffic on his way to the *Vetal Tekdi,* Mitch Shelby had put several things in motion. After his visit with Director Osborne, Mitch had all the necessary permissions to override normal protocols and procedures. His first priority was to seal any possible leaks so as not to cause panic. It was essential to keep this under tight control. If the Indian authorities were to discover loose nuclear material on their soil, brought over albeit inadvertently by a CIA operative, it would be an end to the thaw in the Indo-US relationship for years to come. Mitch had called Freddie Solomon, the station chief for the Indian sub-continent, before he had met with the director. He placed a call to Freddie again.

The secured line between Langley and New Delhi came to life.

"Hello Freddie, this is Mitch Shelby on priority one." Mitch said, his urgency and anxiety spilling over in his speech.

Freddie challenged with a computer generated phrase and Mitch replied with the appropriate answer.

As part of setting up a priority one communication session, each party had to identify themselves using strong identification parameters which involved both biometric information and secret passwords only they knew. Each party was then given a phrase that had to be woven in the first twenty seconds of conversation to further authenticate each party on the already secured channel established using the most advanced encryption technology.

"Freddie, I just met with director Osborne as you know." Mitch continued further. "I need to get your take on the chatter your informants have reported. We keep hearing the nuclear waste was put in the small container and sometimes we hear that it's a hoax. What do you think?"

"Well . . ." Freddie cleared his throat.

He was a cautious man. When the director is involved, he had to be very careful. Freddie's pet peeve was the fact that the intelligence he could gather was quite unreliable at times. Nobody in the CIA appreciated that fact. Everyone needed information, even though it may be accompanied with warnings of low degree of confidence in its authenticity. People just latched on to the information that suited their purpose and conveniently overlooked any warnings as to its reliability.

"Mitch, I would say there is a good chance that the portable North Korean container you speak of actually has the dirty nuclear material in it." Freddie's voice was shaking as he relayed the information. Sitting in New Delhi, he had a far more accurate pulse of how the Indians would react if they found out. An all out war between India and Pakistan was not out of the question. He continued to speak. "What we hear is that the instructions to include or not include the nuclear material in the canister were reversed a few times. So our informants thought one way and then changed the story."

The information Freddie was relaying was quite new. It was almost near real-time relay, so he had to stop and synthesize many pieces in his own head and speak of his conclusions. He continued. "As a result I am not one hundred percent sure. But then we never are, as you well know."

Mitch knew it. But this was no time to play politics or to cover one's behind.

"Freddie, we need to do everything to call off any American sub-contractors we may have on this case." Mitch said as a matter of fact. "There has been a breach. Someone in the Pentagon may have hijacked my operation. Use your local contacts. Override whatever may have been set in motion. My agent is to be left alone. Do you understand? These are the director's orders."

There was urgency and authority in Mitch Shelby's voice that even he was surprised to hear.

LOS ALAMOS, NEW MEXICO:

The head scientist of the nuclear non-proliferation division, Dr. Jones, was woken up in the early morning hours. He was asked to quickly gather a team of scientists specialized in tracing loose nuclear material, specifically from North Korea. Traditionally, the ex-Soviet states received a lot of scrutiny. The Nunn-Lugar Nuclear Threat Initiative had focused on the newly formed nations in Central Asia after collapse of the Soviet Union. But the A.Q. Khan nexus of nuclear market had tentacles in North Korea, Iran, Libya and a few other undesirable places. The NSA and the CIA were acutely aware of it and had staffed enough nuclear scientists who would train the IAEA inspectors. IAEA, the international body that was supposed to have oversight was often not funded properly or lacked the same enthusiasm as the U.S. authorities. So the U.S. had voluntarily helped in this area. The U.S. had a vast database of nuclear material signatures, telltale markings, and pictures of equipment used. Being a nuclear cop required some very specialized knowledge, and Los Alamos was the best place where such knowledge was housed.

The team of scientists had gathered in a large conference room. The room was equipped with a high resolution display on one wall. This morning the display was connected to the military network which could bring in images from satellites. The satellite operators were located at a secret location somewhere in Nevada. They were in a state of readiness to start sending images as soon as their subject was in range. In the last fifteen minutes, a group of ten scientists, carrying their laptops and coffee mugs had trickled in. They were seated and had their laptops open and active. There was quiet excitement in the room. The news of loose nuclear material afoot was enough to wake up everyone assembled there. Their job was to keep track of everything when it came to nuclear technology.

The chief scientist briefly told them what they were about to see.

CHAPTER 38

Sid drove his stolen motorcycle on the narrow road leading up to the *Vetal Tekdi*. He had been on this road many times before. He reached the parking lot at the end of the road, beyond which vehicles were not allowed. From the parking lot he would have to climb another three hundred feet to reach the top. The vertical climb was not much, but the trail was gradual and winding and therefore took much longer to reach the top as compared to a direct climb.

He had made good time riding from Symbiotic Research Labs to this parking lot. There still was at least thirty minutes of daylight left. He had to hurry to reach the top and find a secluded spot, away from prying eyes. Sid parked the motorcycle on its kick stand and removed his helmet keeping it on the handlebar. He removed his backpack from the motorcycle carrier and flung it on his shoulders. He adjusted the backpack straps for better fit. The canister he had picked up from the Symbiotic Labs auditorium was heavy. Besides knowing that it potentially contains harmful material, Sid was extra careful to ensure that the backpack wouldn't slip off. He also made sure that his laptop was in the backpack and that his phone had enough battery charge left.

Moving quickly from the parked motorcycle, Sid broke into a trot towards the trail. There were several hikers and families around the starting point of the trail where the climb became steeper. Nobody paid any special attention to him as Sid started the climb at a hurried pace.

His phone rang. Sid looked up the caller id and realized it was Brad. Sid's heart started to beat even faster. He was told explicitly by Mitch Shelby to not talk to Brad. *Was Brad secretly working for someone else?* Sid knew that Brad could easily obtain Sid's current location by getting someone in the local mobile phone provider's operations to triangulate on Sid's phone. Sid decided to turn off the phone to avoid detection at least for the next twenty minutes until he reached the top.

It was a good precaution on Sid's part, because at his Langley office, Brad was cursing under his breath. He was trying to reach Sid. Something had gone terribly wrong. Anand, Sid's driver was not responding and nor was Sid picking up the phone. Ever since agreeing to work with Oliver Martin, Brad had been increasingly getting worried. What sounded like a good idea a few weeks ago didn't seem so right now. Brad remembered the conversation he had with Oliver Martin exactly six weeks ago. Through some mutual professional and personal contacts, he was approached by Mr. Martin. The two had met in the Manasas National Battlefield Park, away from the usual beltway meeting places.

He remembered Mr. Martin introducing himself. Brad already knew about Oliver Martin and admired him. Brad believed that his country was in the hands of incompetent people. Someone has to do something about that, he had often thought.

He was elated to meet Oliver Martin in person.

"I have been an admirer for a long time. I am ready to help in whatever way I can. The United States of America deserves no less." Brad said politely, bowing a little while he shook hand with Oliver Martin.

Oliver had done his homework and knew that Brad was close to being signed up for the cause. His intermediaries had also told Oliver that Brad was a little worried about circumventing the proper chain of command when it came right down to it. So Oliver proceeded to soften up his new recruit.

"Well Brad, as you know, our beloved country is supposed to be a republic. This notion of one man one vote has never been a part of our Constitution."

Oliver Martin was on his soap box.

"In fact the only people who could vote in the early days were the land owners. And they needed to possess sufficient means to travel in order to reach a voting place."

Oliver had rehearsed these arguments a thousand times before and he could deliver them effectively to a lesser intellectual. At the end of a half-hour, mostly one sided conversation, Brad was convinced that he should sign up.

That was then, but now he was having second thoughts. Brad didn't mind supplying information to Oliver and his group. However, there were worrisome developments out in the field. Brad had heard from his contacts in India that someone was strong arming Sid's driver and the latest news was totally shocking. Sid's driver Anand was dead, murdered in an execution style, by a single bullet in the forehead. And Sid wasn't answering his phone. Nor had Sid checked in with Brad on their pre-arranged schedule in the last twenty-four hours.

Philosophy and political views aside, Brad had a sense of ownership and camaraderie with his trainees. He hoped Sid was safe. Brad thought for a while and then he made up his mind. He must come clean. He had to go and see Mitch Shelby in person.

CHAPTER 39

Sid reached the top. There were a few people around the temple, but for most part the area was deserted. No one wanted to wait there until dark and be caught in an uncomfortable situation of getting lost or getting mugged.

Sid found a spot away from trees and quickly opened up his laptop. He needed the GPS device built in his laptop to give him accurate coordinates. While the laptop was booting up, he got out his mobile phone, turned it on and dialed the number Mitch Shelby had given him.

"Mr. Shelby?" he spoke in the phone. "Yes sir, this is Sid Joshi. I am at an elevation of about five hundred feet from the Pune city street level."

"Well done Sid. I can't tell you how much we all appreciate what you are doing."

Mitch was relieved to hear Sid was safe and at a spot where the scientists would be able to see what he had. Mitch continued to give further instructions.

"I am going to patch in our experts who want to look at the container you have. So please place it on a clean dark surface as quickly as you can."

Sid straddled his phone between his left ear and chin to free up both hands. He then very carefully took the container out of his backpack. He got a good look at what it was in the natural light. As he remembered from the first look in the Symbiotic Labs auditorium, it was a cylindrical container, about eighteen inches long and four inches in diameter. It was quite heavy for its size, perhaps due to its thick metal walls. Sid emptied his backpack, put it on a nearby rock and patted it flat, placing the container on it. The container had several markings as he remembered. In the bright daylight, he could see them better and they looked like a script of one of the Far East languages.

His laptop was powered up and ready. Sid started the GPS application on his laptop. The screen immediately flashed the accurate latitude and longitude of his location. The CIA installed GPS was accurate within a meter. Sid read out the display to Mitch who immediately typed the information in his computer.

Mitch was in contact with the Los Alamos team on a separate phone. He did not want to have Sid involved in the conversation with the scientists. There was no point in overburdening this young agent.

Mitch also had a team on standby to locate and control the appropriate military satellites to zoom in on Sid's location. Mitch muted Sid's line. He carefully relayed the coordinates Sid had given him to the satellite surveillance team.

The large, high definition screen at Los Alamos came to life with images of Sid and the backpack. The image slowly zoomed in and focused on the container Sid had placed on his backpack. Clarity of the image was extraordinary. There was a collective gasp from the scientist as they got a good look at the object of their interest. Many of them immediately started punching keys on their individual laptops. There was a large collection of photographs, indexed and annotated for quick lookup. Apparently a few of them found a match and exclaimed something in excitement. They signaled their chief scientist to have the container rotated to look at the other side of it. He in turn spoke to Mitch and Mitch relayed the instructions to Sid.

The daylight would fade away in another ten minutes. Mitch thought as Sid rotated the cylinder by ninety degrees and repeated the action again when Mitch asked him to.

The military satellite was also taking high-resolution photographs of the container. The scientists would need to catalog the photographs in their collection. But they had to reach a preliminary conclusion fast. Two of the scientists could read, write and speak the Korean language. They were also most familiar with the North Korean stockpile, the technology used, and many other pieces of classified information.

The other scientists huddled around the two. They all looked at images the two were sharing on their laptops. There was an animated discussion. The chief scientists also joined them for the final few minutes of discussion. Then he spoke in the phone.

"Mr. Shelby, we think we have an answer for you." said the chief scientist.

"Stay on the line please." Mitch answered.

His voice was thick with anxiety. He wanted to know what the scientists thought, but he must let Sid pack up and leave. There was a strong possibility that one of his pursuers would catch up with him and seize the container.

"Sid, you can pack up and leave now. We have had a good look at the container and we have taken several photographs." Mitch instructed. "But keep this in mind. Do not, I repeat, do not contact anyone." Mitch couldn't have been more emphatic. Keep your phone charged but turned off. Turn it on in exactly one hour. I will contact you then. And above all else, keep that container covered, in your backpack and do not let it out of your sight. Do not drop it or place it near a source of heat or vibrations. You may be in danger from the people who were following you. The Indian authorities may also look for you, but we will do our best to take care of that angle."

Sid was exhausted. His face showed dark clouds of anxiety as he heard the words.

Mitch continued to speak. "Try not to trace back your path. Find another way to go somewhere other than your apartment. I wish I could send you help. But for now, you are on your own."

Sid turned off the phone. Mitch Shelby's words were still ringing in Sid's ears as he packed away the container. Since he couldn't go back to the motorcycle, he had to find another way to get down. Sid had explored the area before and knew that if he walked long enough, away from the trail he took to come up, he'd hit some part of the city. He wasn't sure which part, and from the instructions he had just heard, it didn't really matter. He couldn't go to his apartment. The question was, what to do next? He didn't know anybody in Pune. His aunt lived in Mumbai, so that was the logical choice. His work at the Symbiotic Research Lab was essentially over whether he liked it or not. He would be implicated in his driver's murder, the theft of a motorcycle, and the possession of a bomb. None of this was going to reflect well on him. But his immediate concern was to get away from his current location.

Sid flung the backpack on his right shoulder and then put his left arm through the other strap. He remembered an old abandoned quarry that was north east of the *Vetal Tekdi* temple. He quickly started walking towards the quarry.

Daylight had almost disappeared but he could see enough to follow the trail. He reached the quarry in ten minutes. He went around taking the east rim of the huge depression where the quarry used to be. Another half hour of walking and climbing down brought him to a part of the city cluttered with low income housing. He walked the narrow lanes, making his way through the now thickening crowd of people in a local street market selling vegetables and fruits. He got curious stares from the shoppers as he made his way through them. In another two hundred meters he spotted an auto rickshaw.

"Pune station." Sid told the driver as he sat down.

He was grateful to take the load off his legs. He placed the backpack beside him and looked at his watch. Twenty more minutes before he had to turn on his phone. Sid sat back, looping his hand through the straps of his backpack. The high pitch noise of the sputtering rickshaw engine had a soothing effect on his tired mind and body. He decided to take a short nap to preserve his stamina.

CHAPTER 40

Ever since her last conversation with Sid, Sarah was consumed by worry. As Sid had asked her to do, she had promptly called Professor Levine who had assured her that everything will be taken care of. But why didn't Sid call back?

Sarah had waited exactly one hour and had tried to call him several times. But Sid had not answered. She remembered her conversation with Sid at the Italian restaurant in Ithaca. She had teased him about the CIA job and killing bad guys. It had seemed funny at the time, but it wasn't funny anymore.

She didn't know whom to ask for help. She didn't know anybody in the Washington D.C. area and didn't want to call her mom or sister to talk about this by phone. Calling Professor Levine again so soon didn't sound like a good idea either. Sarah could barely sleep that night. She left for work early next morning. She was working on another assignment and an early morning war room exercise was planned. She was grateful for it as it allowed her to take her mind off the last night's phone conversation and think of something else. The work session was over by nine thirty. Everyone left the war room quickly, but Sarah stayed there. She felt exhausted and scared. Apparently her inner feelings were spilling out on to her face.

"Ms. Johansson, are you okay?"

Sarah was startled by Todd's query. Todd was passing by and noticed Sarah in the war room. He immediately realized from her face that something was terribly wrong.

"I am fine, thank you." Sarah replied, looking embarrassed.

"No you are not." said Todd, pushing aside chairs in his way to approach her.

Chairs in the war room were scattered everywhere, evidence of animated group discussions that had taken place earlier that morning. The large white board was full of figures and phrases and some yellow sticky notes were pasted on the board. The firm had a strict policy of not leaving any information in the open including writings on a white board. By protocol, the last person leaving a meeting was responsible for the cleanup. Sarah was obviously that person at this time.

Todd continued to speak as he made his way to the whiteboard and started erasing it. Sarah jumped to her feet and protested.

"Mr. Lester, please let me take care of that."

"Sit down." Todd said without turning back. He continued to methodically clean the whiteboard.

"Is everything okay at home?" he queried.

Sarah remembered what she had seen on Todd's desk. *Did the esoteric scribbling have something to do with Sid's assignment?* But then what possible connection could there be between Sid and her boss? She fought back from her thoughts to regain her composure.

"Yes, everything is fine, thanks." Sarah replied.

"You have a boyfriend overseas in service, right?" Todd asked.

Sarah was surprised. "Yes I have a very close friend overseas. He is in India, not serving in the armed forces but working for some other government agency."

Sarah was wondering how Todd would know about Sid. But then again, all the new recruits knew everything about each other and talked non-stop. They put information up on many social networking web sites. Todd could have easily heard conversations around him. Sarah knew that Todd Lester had a long, distinguished career with the Pentagon. She decided to reach out for help. Besides she remembered the circled words 'Symbiotic Research Labs' in Todd's scribbled notes from her earlier visit to his office.

"Mr. Lester . . ." Sarah started to speak and hesitated.

Todd turned around, surprised by her voice laden with emotions. He looked at her carefully. His face showed sympathy and concern.

"What is it Sarah? Something is bothering you. Out with it." He commanded her in an avuncular tone. Todd pulled a chair and sat down next to her.

Sarah started to talk. She was careful not to give out more information than needed to explain her anxiety. She told Todd that Sid was part of a scientific team working at a company called Symbiotic Research Labs in India. She also related how she had reached out to Sid to get some basic information for her report on the embedded chip market research.

Todd listened carefully trying to keep a poker face.

"Is Sid working for Symbiotic Research Labs or is he working for a U.S. based company?" Todd asked.

Sarah didn't want to answer his question. But in her vulnerable mental state she had blurted out inconsistent information. It would be obvious to anybody that she was either lying or withholding information. She struggled to come up with a make believe response, but realized it was futile.

"Sid works for the CIA." she said lowering her voice.

Todd couldn't keep his composure anymore. His mind had raced to digest information he was hearing, connecting it to the whole affair with Roger Patel and Oliver Martin. Todd wasn't aware that Symbiotic Research Labs was of interest to the CIA. This was potentially an explosive development. As he realized the implications of what Sarah was telling him, he became visibly upset. Sarah was surprised by Todd's reaction.

"Sarah, did you say his driver was killed in a shooting?" Todd asked. "And your friend is missing?"

Sarah nodded, silent tears rolling down her cheeks. She was angry inside and wanted to confront Todd about the notes she saw on his desk. But she checked herself. There was no point in confronting her boss. Besides, Todd was sympathetic and nice. *He wasn't involved in anything bad. Or was he?*

Todd was thinking fast. He realized this would be the turning point in his career at Arnold & Gregg. He had been uncomfortable performing some of the things his job had demanded ever since he joined the firm. But he had managed to rationalize a lot of things in his own mind. The fat paycheck helped too. But his participation in the Roger Patel case had made him really uncomfortable. Todd was sure that Roger didn't know even half of what was taking place on his behalf. And he had a notion that even he didn't know what was being orchestrated by Mr. Martin. He started to feel queasy.

Todd recollected the episode when Roger called the front desk and the receptionist could not find either Roger Patel by name or his company, Pinnacle Systems.

Todd had to do something quickly. In its clever way, the firm of Arnold & Gregg had skillfully twisted and obfuscated the client wishes and connected them to an ideologue's agenda which even the firm didn't understand, or didn't want to understand. There would be a windfall of political favors that the firm could use to its fullest advantage in future.

On one occasion Todd had protested to Jim about how things were shaping up in the Roger Patel case. But Jim had firmly put him down. Todd was astute enough to not press on. He was patching things up with Jill and it was all going to work out fine. He knew that Jim would not hesitate to play the trump card of Todd's slip at the Blue Pearl several months ago. And if Jim did that, it would cause irreparable damage to his marriage.

Todd was ashamed of himself for falling prey to Jim's tactics. But things had gone amuck. An innocent person getting killed could never be a part of any deal he was involved in. He must stop it. He didn't care anymore for his job at the firm. He had enough financial security. He didn't have to sell out his morals for a buck.

Todd got up. He pulled several facial tissues from a nearby box of Kleenex. He handed them to Sarah and placed his hand on her shoulder.

"Sarah, don't worry. I know just the right people who can help. In fact, people who must help. And do me a favor. Take a few days off. Go visit your family until I get back to you with some news."

Something in Todd's voice and his demeanor reassured Sarah. Todd pulled out a small notebook and handed it to her.

"Write down your personal cell phone number." he said. "I will get in touch with a few people and I will call you when I know something."

Sarah felt much better as she gathered her belongings scattered around the war room. As she was ready to leave, a thought came to her mind. She paused in her tracks and suddenly she had an epiphany. She just knew what she must do. She would pack her bags, buy a ticket, and fly to Mumbai, India. She had to find Sid.

CHAPTER 41

New Delhi, India:

Freddie Solomon acted quickly. He made several calls. First and foremost he had to figure out if any of the CIA regular contractors were on the case, either shadowing Sid Joshi or causing him any harm. He had enough clout and budget to reach the right people who controlled the loosely-knit mafia that performed some of CIA's dirty work in the Mumbai area. Freddie put out the word that he would not look kindly to any actions contrary to his wishes. He even put out a reward to stop any rival faction or other elements that might be on this case.

Freddie had cultivated a network of people that he could count on. Among them were influential politicians and bureaucrats. India's huge democratic ship was often put on an even keel by its vast cadre of bureaucrats. Freddie knew that politicians come and go as their fortunes can turn on a dime. However, the highly placed '*babus*', as the bureaucrats were called derisively, were a constant factor in the power base of the country.

Secondly, Freddie had to smooth over any issues where Sid may be implicated. The murder investigation of Sid's driver was just starting. The local police were clueless. A special branch of investigators were to be involved because of the proximity of the crime to the internationally important establishment of Symbiotic Research Labs. It wouldn't be difficult to hire a competent attorney who would represent Sid.

LANGLEY, VIRGINIA:

Mitch hung up the phone and looked up to the clock on his office wall. He noted down the time in a notepad on his table. He must call Sid in exactly one hour. He then un-muted the phone line to Los Alamos.

"Dr. Jones, are you there?" Mitch said.

"Yes Mr. Shelby." Dr. Edward Jones, the chief scientist replied.

Since watching images of the nuclear material storage container on the large screen, he had huddled with his scientists. The group of ten nuclear physicists and researchers was gathered around him. They had exchanged notes and were talking excitedly. Just as Mitch came back on line, the group had reaffirmed their initial consensus.

"So, what's your assessment Dr. Jones?" Mitch asked. He was afraid to hear a reply.

"We have seen such container before. I am afraid it is from the stockpile of spent nuclear fuel from North Korea." Dr. Jones stated as a matter of fact.

It was no secret that U.S. spy agencies had acted aggressively to collect as much information as they could about the North Korean nuclear program. While diplomats were talking to the North Korean regime in the nineties, U.S. nuclear scientists dedicated to the non-proliferation effort had slowly collected a vast amount of information about North Korea's nuclear technology, locations of their facilities, and even pictures of the facilities and warehouses.

"The container has distinctive markings that are consistent with our information. It tells us that it is a storage device the North Koreans use for spent nuclear material."

Mitch sighed. He was afraid of the answer. But he needed to find out all he could.

"How much can this container hold? And what sort of damage can it cause?" he pressed Dr. Jones for more details.

"That's the unusual thing." continued Dr. Jones. "The container can hold enough material to be a dirty nuclear bomb. It's nothing like a bomb that detonates a strong charge to cause nuclear fusion, you know."

Dr. Jones was cautious. He didn't want any non-scientists to get a wrong impression and take some action based on it. "Let me be very clear. What we term as a dirty nuclear bomb is concentration of enough radioactive material that can spread dangerous levels of radioactivity. Now let me also say."

Mitch had no time for a cautious and slow conversation. He cut off Dr. Jones. "I am sorry to interrupt, but is it dangerous enough to cause widespread mortality? And if so, to what extent? And what do you mean by unusual thing?" Mitch snapped. He needed answers fast.

Dr. Jones could feel the pressure Mitch was under.

"The container seems to be fitted with a timer assisted release mechanism, perhaps using a small explosive charge. The unusual thing is that we don't think North Koreans have fitted such a device. This looks like an add-on in the aftermarket."

Mitch was getting extremely uncomfortable. He thought, *why am I, a digital security expert, discussing nuclear black market add on devices?*

But he realized, whether he liked it or not, he was involved now and must deal with it.

"If detonated, what's the damage it can cause? Give me approximate area of coverage and severity of the radioactive fallout." Mitch really wanted the bottom line.

Dr. Jones spoke with a heavy voice. "Our estimate is that, and mind you it's only an educated guess. Well, we think the fallout could spread to fifteen or twenty city blocks in a matter of minutes."

Mitch was stunned. He listened for another minute, thanked Dr. Jones, and hung up. He sat back in his chair. There were dark circles around his tired eyes.

He must alert Director Osborne right away.

PUNE, INDIA:

"Pune station aa gaya sir"

Sid awoke from his nap. The rickshaw driver was telling him that they had reached the destination of Pune Railway station. Sid took out some bills and put them in driver's hand as he exited the rickshaw keeping a firm grip on his backpack. The bus station was next to the railway station. Sid walked to the bus station and purchased a ticket to Mumbai. The bus would leave in another fifteen minutes and his seat was reserved. Sid bought a bottle of cold water and looked at his watch. It was time to turn on his cell phone.

There were several groups of families, all apparently related to each other, travelling on his bus. The women and children were engaged in animated cross talk, while the men had gathered near the bus door smoking and talking politics. Sid's phone rang exactly when expected. There was no recognizable caller identification.

"Hello?" Sid spoke, hoping it was Mitch Shelby. It was.

"Sid, how are you?" Mitch asked.

It wasn't a small talk. Mitch wanted to know how Sid was taking all this. The last thing he wanted was a green field agent, actually a non-agent, giving up under extreme pressure. And considering Sid was really recruited for the job as a computer scientist, it would have been understandable if he was cracking under pressure.

"I am just tired." Sid said and continued. "So what is this container I am carrying? Is it a bomb? Scot had talked about activating it, but I am positive he had not done so before I got hold of it." Sid said all this in one breath.

"Slow down Sid." Mitch said. "I am a good friend of your professor Levine. He tells me you are a tough kid. Don't give up easily." Mitch wanted to encourage Sid. Mention of Professor Levine had the desired effect on Sid. His anxiety came down a notch. "We certainly don't want you to give up now. It may sound like a cliché but your country really needs you right now." Mitch implored Sid.

"I am not giving up on anything. But I want some answers." Sid was scared and annoyed at the same time. "When I signed up for the job, it was not for any of these adventures. I am a computer scientist. And they killed my driver. They were following me like maniacs."

Sid's throat was dry from breathing dust on the *Vetal Tekdi* trail. He took a sip of water. "Who are these people? And who is Scot? How did he know I was carrying this bomb, when even I didn't know it? And without my knowledge I did carry it to the Symbiotic campus. Who put it in my backpack? Who the hell was my driver really working for?" Sid vented through his many questions.

Sid's raised voice was attracting unwanted attention from some of the men talking politics.

"*Aare ye to kuch bomb shomb bola re.*" said one of the men.

Sid flashed a friendly smile towards the men and indicated by gestures he was talking to someone crazy at the other end of his conversation. That did the trick. The men smiled back and turned their attention to discussing politics again.

"Sid, please accept my sincere apology. I will explain everything to you, but you must listen to me right now and turn off your phone immediately after our conversation." Mitch tried to placate Sid. He now had to lie to Sid so as to not panic him. "The container in your backpack is not a bomb in conventional sense. It's a container for storing spent nuclear material."

Mitch was not a smooth liar and he knew it. He had to make it brief and not say too much. But he had to be convincing enough so Sid would trust him and follow his instructions.

"It is perfectly safe unless the container is opened. If opened, there will be low grade radioactivity in the immediate vicinity covering less than ten thousand square feet. That's roughly a circle of less than sixty feet radius."

Sid was listening intently. He had surmised something on these lines on his own anyways. But knowing the fact that it was a very low grade radioactive material gave him much needed reassurance.

"Regardless of its low strength, it'll be a nightmare if the Indian authorities even get a hint of this. Do you understand me?" Mitch continued. "Where are you now?"

"I am about to board a bus to Mumbai." Sid replied. "I don't know where I can go if not to my apartment. I have a relative in Mumbai. So I am planning to go there."

Mitch was relieved again. It sounded like Sid was not too rattled to do something stupid.

"That's perfect, Sid. We'll take care of everything. Here is a storyline you need to stick to, okay?"

Mitch talked for another ten minutes as Sid listened. Sid was to be on a vacation. Events at the Symbiotic campus would be taken care of. But the Indian authorities would surely follow him closely at least for couple of weeks. So Sid must keep an appearance of someone on a vacation. He was to pick a location as Mitch explained in detail. Sid was to convince his relatives to travel with him instead of travelling alone, to make it look like a family vacation.

Mitch had not revealed that perhaps ISI operatives would also try to follow him to recover the container. He would have to lean hard on the Pentagon leaders running the Pakistan policy. With direct involvement of the director of the CIA and a nod from the President, it should be achievable, Mitch thought.

The bus driver honked to warn passengers it was time to leave. Sid looked up. Most of the passengers had made a bee line to board the bus. He started to walk and spoke in the phone.

"My bus is about to leave. I understand what I need to do. Once I reach Mumbai, I will get another phone and use my personal email account to make contact."

"Good luck Sid, and I'll make it up to you when we get out of this crisis, I promise you." Mitch said.

"Thanks." Sid said as he climbed the steps to enter the bus, hung up the call and turned off his phone.

CHAPTER 42

General Iqbal Chaudhry was longing for female company. He wished he could visit his club where standing arrangements were made for what he needed. It was a discreet place that looked after its clients' every need, from a game of squash to social and private escort service of personal choosing.

As much as he longed for the release, he could not afford to visit the club. He had not driven anywhere by himself for as long as he could remember. Driving himself to the club just did not feel right. Besides this big mess he had created had to be sorted out first.

The act of betrayal by his orderly was hard to swallow. General Chaudhry had always held himself as a good judge of character. And he was. To rise up in an institution like army there were two requirements. First was to have very large coattails of a leader one is loyal to and second was to possess an uncanny knack to find people one could trust and nurture to follow and support you. The General was lucky in the former and had developed a keen sense of people for the latter. He truly believed that his orderly would have given his life to protect him.

But the old equations of loyalty and of patriotism were being corrupted. Challenging the Taliban, even half-heartedly, was like disturbing a hornet's nest. The backlash was overwhelming, ferocious, and widespread. Even the ISI had miscalculated penetration of the Taliban in the Pakistani society. The fact that his own orderly was coerced into betrayal was a testament to the changing realities in his country.

He had to recover the dirty bomb quickly, before a major war broke out which would undoubtedly have large number of casualties on both sides. And it would do irreparable damage to both sides. He often thought of his father who had told him stories of their home in Delhi. General Chaudhry had always discerned a hint of nostalgia and affection whenever his father spoke of their old neighborhood, and their Hindu friends. The bond his father shared with them when discussing poetry, politics and their opposition of the British rule was unmistakable in his voice.

But the story had gone sour after the partition. Unspeakable atrocities and hatred had spilled over, resulting in mass hysteria and violence. The waves of that violence had swept his father and his family, including little Iqbal, to the shores of Pakistan. He still remembered the panicked and sudden departure from his home. He had still not completely overcome the sense of fear and loss, being uprooted from his home in that fashion.

Prolonged uncertainty of his sister's whereabouts and her presumed death that the family grudgingly accepted had dealt a devastating blow to his father. During their train journey with just the belongings they could carry with them, a mob of Hindus had set fire to the train. In the chaos that ensued, his sister was separated from the family. They never saw her again and presumed she was killed in the melee. The scar of losing a family member had never healed, even after all these years.

His father had worked hard in the new country. He made himself a wealthy man again and sent Iqbal to England for higher secondary and college education. Iqbal had shown interest in an army career, which was easy to arrange with his father's connections.

General Chaudhry pushed aside his thoughts. Since his wife's death, he had become prone to be sentimental. That was a weakness for an army man. But he was also seeing futility of the current course of the strategy being followed by Islamabad. Making peace with India would be a wise move. And moving towards the path of true democracy and secularism would in fact lead to prosperity. He was convinced of that.

But his immediate goal was to recover the dirty bomb to make sure it was returned safely back to where it was stolen from.

His man Hafez was reliable. He had to count on him to recover the bomb. His instructions to Hafez were clear and Hafez would follow them to a tee. General Chaudhry walked to a chest of drawers in his office and opened the top drawer. Inside, there were several phones tucked neatly in their charging units. He examined the labels against each, picked up one phone and pressed a speed dial key.

"It's me." he whispered as Hafez picked up at the other end in Pune. "*Kya Khabar hai?*" he inquired. His voice was authoritative and showed he was in control. He was inquiring of Hafez's progress. "Have you followed the CIA mercenaries you talked about?"

"Yes sir, we followed them. They were watching one scientist at the Symbiotic Labs. They followed him and so did we." Hafez said. And then his voice turned apologetic. "But sir, this scientist was riding a motorcycle like a possessed man. We lost him in the thick Pune traffic."

"You bloody fool. How could you not follow a stupid scientist?" the General demanded. "Go find where he lives. He must have the container with him. No wait. If he is our man and has the container with him, then he will not go home." *Where will he go?* The General thought.

General Chaudhry continued to think for a minute. He went through several possibilities in his mind, trying to walk in the shoes of a novice agent who must be under a lot of pressure. "He must be headed for Mumbai. If his profile is right, he will most likely hand over the container to another CIA man travelling from the U.S. I don't think the CIA will want the Indians to know."

"Yes sir, so what should we do?" Hafez asked.

"Go to Mumbai and check out all hotels near the airport. Look for an American who has just arrived. And look for this scientist fellow too." said the General.

"*Samaz gaya sir.*" Hafez replied.

"And Hafez, whatever happens, don't get caught. And don't do any killings. Just get the damn container and call me."

CHAPTER 43

Konkan is a region of India known for its natural beauty and bounty of its exotic fruits. Northern *Konkan*, which is in the state of Maharashtra, is a narrow strip of land that starts about forty kilometers due south of Mumbai, hugging the Arabian Sea on its west flank. It extends southwards for three hundred kilometers to the city of *Sindhu Durg*, meaning a sea fortress. On the east is the edge of the Deccan Plateau, rising some two thousand feet from sea level, which separates *Konkan* from the flat and fertile land that is part of the state of Maharashtra.

Konkan had been a topic of conversation in the Joshi household for many years. Sid's father, Vasant Joshi, was very fond of *Konkan* as it was the land of his ancestors. Although Vasant had been to *Konkan* only a few times as a tourist, it had made quite an impression on him. Vasant was from a community called *Kokanastha Bramhins*, meaning literally Brahmins from the land of *Konkan*. The community was characterized by people of light skin and light eye color, making them visually stand apart from most of the Indian people. Sid had inherited the same light complexion and light blue eye color. He had always wanted to visit *Konkan*, although none of the family trips had allowed them enough time to pull it off.

"*Lonavala*, the bus will stop here for ten minutes and no more." The bus driver warned his passengers and opened the bus door.

Sid was woken up from his deep slumber. *Why was he thinking of Konkan? Or was he dreaming?* In time of extreme pressure people are known to hallucinate as a defense mechanism. *Was he hallucinating?* He stretched his neck and shoulders. And then he realized. His mind was still working while his body got some rest. *Konkan* was right off the Arabian Sea so it would be a perfect vacation spot, consistent with what Mitch had instructed him to find. *He would ask his aunt to direct him to a place in Konkan,* he thought to himself. With that decision, Sid felt like a weight was lifted off his shoulders.

His fellow travelers got up and made a line towards the bus door. Sid wanted to just sleep. The past twelve hours had been extraordinarily difficult. That fact combined with his lonely existence far away from home and friends had reached a tipping point. He wanted to quit the job and go back home. He yearned for the peace and quiet of his home in Birmingham and the loving company of his parents.

Wouldn't it be nice to take a relaxing vacation in Konkan with mom and dad? Sid thought.

But he was neck deep in a precarious situation. Even calling his parents may be dangerous to them. Besides he knew they would freak out if they knew what he was carrying in his backpack.

Any sane person would freak out, he thought to himself, and chuckled in spite of the grim situation he was in.

Does it make me insane or I am freaking out and not realizing it?

Sid often carried out dialogues in his head when he was working on a difficult problem or was faced with a dilemma. In his college work, while other students were working hard on a take home assignment or term papers, preparing multiple drafts, rewriting and discarding answers, Sid was usually very quiet and still. He usually finished his term papers or take-home tests in one sitting and aced them. In his first semester, his classmates thought that Sid had frozen with fear at the finals, and was going to fail. But Sid worked everything out in his head and when he was ready, took ten minutes to write down his answers and walk out. He had pulled a A minus grade in that course.

The cog wheels in his head were spinning fast now. This was unlike any test he had taken. Mitch had told him to find a relatively isolated spot along India's vast coastline for the transfer. Sid's cover should be a relaxing vacation. Mitch would arrange communication with the folks in Symbiotic Research Labs and of course he would smooth everything over with respect to Sid's driver's death.

But there was something that bothered Sid the most. There was a possibility that some foreign agents may try to recover the dirty nuclear bomb he was carrying. Since the explosion at the Symbiotic Research Labs was thwarted by Sid, the people who planned this act must be furious and would try everything they could to recover the bomb.

No, he must not let that happen. He will not let that happen. Sid's jaw tightened as it usually did when he was resolved to do something. His lacrosse teammates had seen that face when Sid inspired his team in many come from behind wins. And Sarah had seen it too when they were getting ready to better their own record in the last stretch of few half-marathons they had run.

The bus driver and his fellow passengers returned from the break. The bus resumed its run towards Mumbai, now going downhill on the winding roads of the Western Ghat, climbing down the Deccan Plateau to the sea level. Sid reached a conclusion in his mind. He would not go to his aunt in Mumbai. That would be too risky for her. He would check in a hotel and plan his trip from there. There was a problem though. Prepaid phones were not easily available to walk-in customers. Due to India's perennial problems with many acts of terrorism, the government had instituted rigorous verification processes that all telecom operators had to follow. Sid would have to ask for a favor and get a prepaid phone from his aunt.

The bus reached *Dadar*, a busy suburb of Mumbai. It was the last stop. Sid got down, clutching his backpack carefully. He had not packed any clothes or toiletries. Travelling to another city was of course not on the agenda when he started his day that morning. He would have to make a stop at his aunt's against his wishes, but he would give her an excuse and make it a short visit to cover his clothes purchases and to get a phone.

Sid was reasonably sure that no one had followed him. Ever since getting off the highway riding the stolen motorcycle, his route had been so unpredictable even to himself, that nobody would have guessed where he was going. Unless somebody at Langley or Los Alamos was a mole, and had passed on his coordinates, no one could possibly guess. And the existence of his aunt was not in the CIA database. Even if someone approached his parents on a false pretext to get such information, they would never give out such information. He was reasonably sure of that too.

It was dark outside. But true to what he had heard, Mumbai was not sleeping just yet. He would get a taxi to his aunt's place, spend the night there and figure out tomorrow a course of action. His aunt no doubt would cajole him to stay more, but he would make it up to her later.

CHAPTER 44

Sid left his aunt's flat in *Shivaji Park*, a middle-class neighborhood in Dadar, thanking her profusely for her help. She had taken him to nearby shops the next morning where he bought clothes and other necessities in a hurry. She had an extra mobile phone. She insisted that he should borrow it for however long he needed. The phone came with a prepaid plan with enough balance and the ability to make calls overseas.

Sid felt guilty to cut his visit short and was amazed once again by the power of family ties. The aunt he had not seen or talked to for years had welcomed him with open arms and genuine affection. He had used her to get what he wanted quickly. But there was no alternative in the given situation. Besides, if anyone was following him, he didn't want them to focus on his aunt so he had to move on.

Sid took a taxi to a hotel near the airport. He only knew a few hotels in Mumbai and they all were near the Mumbai International Airport, so it wasn't difficult to make up his mind as to where to go. His aunt had given him an address of a hotel in *Konkan* and had promised to make a booking for him. Sid had lied to her that he and a friend were going on this trip as his aunt insisted that he not go alone.

Sid checked in, told the bell boy that he had no luggage and took an elevator to his floor. He entered his room and gingerly put down the backpack. The backpack had become an appendage, a part of his body over the last many hours. He wished it away. He couldn't wait for this chapter of his training to be over and be back in Washington D.C. area. The first thing he would do would be to call Sarah and have a nice dinner, most likely at an Italian restaurant. It brought back memories of their dinner in Ithaca. He wanted to pick up their relationship from where he had left. Sid had talked to her several times since his graduation, and he was certain that their feelings for each other were still the same. And now Sarah had a job in Washington D.C. *How wonderful is that,* he thought.

He had a new phone that nobody knew about. But what if someone was tracing all calls to Sarah's phone? You could never be too sure. He was entangled in the serious business of a dirty nuclear bomb. Against all his emotions, he would not make that call to Sarah. In fact he was resolved to not even call Mitch Shelby until the very last minute that he must. Mitch knew where he was and knew the geography of India. He must already be making arrangements for a Navy SEAL unit to be ready to drop in at a moment's notice. In fact someone in the United States Navy must already be on notice, Sid thought to himself.

He had not eaten well in the last twenty four hours, and thought of checking out restaurants in the hotel. Even though he had a reservation at the hotel in *Konkan*, he had to arrange for a car. He would do that at the travel desk in the hotel lobby. A rented car in India always came with a driver which suited him just fine. Sid had no desire of getting used to the left hand drive cars or the Indian traffic rules.

Sid took an elevator to the lobby, picked up a travel brochure and made his way towards the front desk as he was browsing it.

"How can we help you sir?" A pleasant voice inquired.

Sid looked up. A petite front desk receptionist was smiling at him.

"I need a car for a trip to." Sid fumbled and searched his pockets to get a paper his aunt had written on. "For a trip to *Murud* beach in *Konkan*." He completed.

"Of course, sir. If you go to the travel desk, they will take care of you." Said the receptionist and she pointed to a flight of stairs.

"It's down those steps on the mezzanine floor. Is there anything else I can help you with?"

"No, thanks." Sid said and turned towards the stairs.

As he took a few steps down, he could see the travel desk about thirty feet in front of him, where a young lady was arguing with the concierge.

"But I must go to Pune now. I have to be at the Symbiotic Research Labs. Here is the address. How long is the trip?" The young lady's impatient American accent rang through the open area.

Sid felt as if he was in suspended reality. Everything around him went out of focus, the chatter of hotel guests around him seemed to be coming from a vast distance. Because that voice he heard was unmistakably familiar. *Was he going crazy? Was the ordeal he was going through finally taking its toll?*

Sid swallowed hard and looked ahead carefully.

That has to be Sarah, he said softly as if to convince himself.

The same voice, the same hair, she looked exactly like Sarah from the back. He must be hallucinating.

Only one way to find out, he said to himself and called out loudly. "Sarah, is that you?"

A few people turned to look who was shouting. And then the young customer at the travel desk turned back, her demeanor quizzical.

Sarah's face showed so many emotions, moving from curious to disbelief to sheer joy, all in the span of the few seconds it took her to realize someone was calling her name and that someone was Sid. Now it was Sarah's turn to disbelieve her faculties. *This person looked like Sid and sounded like him. But was he really? Was her mind playing tricks on her? Was her brain, tired from long travel and consumed by worry, not functioning well anymore?*

But wait, it was Sid. She couldn't take it anymore. Tears started rolling down her cheeks. She wanted to say something, but her throat was choked with emotions. Sid was walking towards her, his face also changing from disbelief to joy. Sarah wanted to run towards him but her legs didn't cooperate.

Sid reached her and held her in his arms affectionately. They stayed embraced a long time. Finally Sid spoke. "What are you doing here? I can't believe you just showed up."

Sarah had recovered her composure. "What do you think?" She said in a scolding voice.

"They say India is a beautiful country to travel to, so I came as a tourist." She said with a straight face. "Now it did cross my mind that I may run into you." She said smiling. Then she turned all serious again. "What the hell is going on Sid? Are you okay? You look terrible."

Sarah had been anxious and angry. Her emotions finally found their way. "When was last time you slept well? And what's this hush-hush mission you are on?" Sarah took steps forward pushing Sid angrily. "I talked to Professor Levine as you told me to, and then you just went AWOL on me." Sarah was now turning angrier and louder.

"Shh . . ." Sid tried to calm her. He pulled her aside and lowered his voice for emphasis. "Sarah, I have got entangled into something terrible; something that I had nothing to do with. But now I am involved and must get out of it." Sid was trying to reason with her. "Let's go upstairs and I will explain. There is so much I want to tell you. But before any of that, there something I have been longing for."

Sid paused and wiped away tears from Sarah's cheeks. He then cupped her face in both his hands and kissed her.

"I love you Sarah. I am so glad you are here." Sid's voice turned a whisper as he said it.

Then his face lit up. "Let me book a car for us. We are going to *Konkan*." He said, his signature mischievous look returning in his eyes.

Sarah felt the tension in her body melt away. She was feeling a sense of calmness that had eluded her over the past forty eight hours. She had no idea what or where *Konkan* was. But with Sid she was ready to go to the end of the world.

CHAPTER 45

They both slept well. In each other's company their anxiety and tension melted away albeit for a short time. It was the much needed peaceful rest Sid had hoped for.

Next morning they were getting ready to leave. The car and the driver were ready outside the hotel lobby. The driver loaded their bags in the trunk of the car but Sid refused to hand over the backpack to him. The driver was not surprised. He routinely used to drive information technology professionals who seldom were ready to part with their laptops.

Sarah had already checked out and waited by the car while Sid started walking towards the hotel lobby to check out.

He scanned the vast drive through area outside where their car was parked and then scanned the hotel lobby as he entered. There were no signs of any suspicious men watching them. He was satisfied and continued to walk through the hotel lobby. As he approached the front desk, he saw the same receptionist girl behind the counter talking to two uniformed policemen. As he entered the lobby, the girl noticed him and pointed to him. The two uniformed police turned and waited as Sid approached the counter.

"Are you Mr. Sid Joshi?" one of the cops asked him.

"Yes I am. Is there something wrong?" Sid tried to speak casually. But he was quite worried inside. His driver was murdered and he had taken off without any explanation. It was expected that the police would catch up with him. *Why did he believe Mitch Shelby would take care of everything?* His backpack was on his shoulder, in plain sight of the police. What if they asked him to open it? What would he do? Running from police was not a wise option. Should he claim diplomatic immunity? Would the U.S. Consulate General in Mumbai back him up?

"Yes, you need to come with us." the other cop said. His English was poor and he looked uncouth.

"But why? What seems to be the problem?" Sid protested.

Sarah was outside near their car, watching through the glass wall and saw the two policemen talking to Sid. From their body language, she sensed that they had hostile intentions. A few minutes back Sarah had noticed the same two cops get down from a rickshaw about hundred yards from the hotel. She had wondered why two official looking policemen were riding a rickshaw for hire. She thought it was unusual but didn't think anything of it.

Sarah entered the lobby and started walking towards the bell captain's desk which was just a few feet away. She asked the man at the desk for hotel security. The bellman wanted to know why, but something on Sarah's face told him to not question her. He picked up the phone, said something, looked across the lobby and nodded to someone.

In the meanwhile, at the front desk, one of the two cops escorted Sid away, outside the earshot of the receptionist and said politely. "Sir, we just have a few questions. We want to make sure your papers are in order."

Sid was surprised. The hotel had asked to see his passport and he had shown it to them. It was a routine in most countries for the foreigners to show their passports to the hotel staff at registration. So why is this policeman asking for papers? There also seemed something out of place with the two of them, although Sid couldn't put his finger on it. Or was the ruse of checking papers a preamble to more thorough questioning later? Sid looked at the receptionist to ask for her help.

Sarah's plan was simple. She wanted the hotel security to interject, giving her a chance to get the backpack from Sid. In

India, a male policeman would not be able to forcibly take away the backpack from her, at least in a public area.

Hafez saw the two hotel security personnel walking towards them. He had acquired two police uniforms from his contacts in Mumbai. Since last night they were pretending to be Mumbai police and going from hotel to hotel near the airport. They only had a name from the intelligence they had received while travelling to Mumbai. Their instructions were to look for one Sid Joshi. It was a long shot to find who they were looking for. But there wasn't any other way. On the highway outside Pune, the CIA mercenaries had lost their subject and so had Hafez and his partner.

General Chaudhry was angry and quite clear in his instructions. When Hafez called him to report lack of progress, the General had told him to stop following the CIA hired men and to focus their search at hotels in Mumbai. The General had assumed that Sid had contacted his chain of command. And obviously they must have been hopping mad at what they heard. He also surmised that some senior CIA official would be meeting Sid in Mumbai, presumably arriving by air and hence his instructions to visit hotels near the airport.

"Don't try any rough business." The General had warned Hafez.

He didn't want Hafez to get caught. If Hafez was caught and broke down, the General himself would be implicated. Besides, the container could still be on the Symbiotic Labs campus or with another CIA operative. The fact that this Sid Joshi had bolted from the Symbiotic campus was pointing all fingers to him. But anything was possible.

Hafez knew he had only few seconds. He mustered all the authority he could gather and talked sternly.

"Are you going somewhere? You can't travel without our permission."

"I am going on vacation." Sid protested. By now Sarah had approached them and the hotel security was ten meters away approaching from the other side.

"We are going on a vacation." Sid repeated himself, this time putting his arm around Sarah for emphasis.

The hotel security knew all the police inspectors in the area. They were puzzled to see two strangers who looked awkward in their ill fitting police uniform. Hafez sensed the problem.

"We are sorry; you can go on vacation with your wife. We will get in touch with you when you return."

With that said, Hafez pulled his partner and they both left in a hurry just as the hotel security approached Sid and Sarah.

"Are you okay madam, sir?" one of the security staff enquired.

"What did the police want?" asked the other.

"Apparently nothing." Sid replied rather confused.

"They wanted to ask me some questions, but said that they will be back when we return from vacation. He didn't even ask when we'll be back."

"I don't think they were Mumbai police. It must be some scam. Our apologies, sir."

"You know the hotel guests are targeted by various scam artists and again we do apologise for this inconvenience."

The security officers were polite and contrite. They left Sid and Sarah.

"I knew those two were not police." Sarah said triumphantly.

She explained to Sid what she had observed. The two had a taste of what can go wrong. Sid hoped that a similar incident doesn't repeat on their way to *Konkan.* They proceeded back to the rental car outside the hotel lobby.

Hafez had to decide what to do next. He had the good fortune of bumping into his quarry. But all indications were that this guy was genuinely on a vacation with his wife or a girlfriend. He would report to General Chaudhry later tonight. For now he must return to Pune and figure out a way to break in the Symbiotic campus. *But where would he begin to look?*

Hafez cursed under his breath. Just as he was leaving the hotel premises, a thought occurred to him. He had to find where Sid was going for vacation, just in case the General wanted him followed. But he couldn't take a chance of reentering the hotel in police uniform. The security personnel would most certainly stop him.

Hafez knew someone, a Pakistan sympathizer he had cultivated for sundry jobs in Mumbai. This person was a bellboy in a nearby luxury hotel. Hafez dialed his number.

"*Aare ustad, kya kar rahe ho?*" Hafez queried.

"*Allah ki marzi se bilkul theek hun. Hamari yaad kaise ki?*" his contact replied, asking Hafez for reason of this call.

They talked for a few minutes. Hafez had to agree to pay five thousand rupees to get the information he wanted. But he was sure that the exact destination and the car's license plate information would be relayed to him in less than an hour.

He would visit one of Mumbai's nice restaurants for lunch. The expense account on this assignment was quite liberal. He smiled to himself as he dragged his partner to the street and hailed a taxi.

CHAPTER 46

Mitch was getting impatient. It had been almost eighteen hours since the last time he spoke with Sid. Mitch was hoping that Sid would not panic and give up. He had talked more with his friend Professor Levine. Richard had assured him that Sid was not a quitter. Mitch hoped his friend was right.

With permission from Director Osborne, Mitch had put into place a plan for a Navy SEAL unit to rendezvous with Sid somewhere along India's coastal waters. The Fifth Fleet was positioned within two hours by fast aircraft from India's western coastline. Assuming that was where Sid was headed, he would signal the naval commander charged with this mission just as soon as he had Sid's precise coordinates.

A lot had happened in the past twenty four hours. Mitch had not slept at all. He was on phone with Freddie Solomon who had shown excellent cooperation and results. Of course with direct orders from the director, backed by presidential authority, things usually moved fast. Freddie had taken care of the entire situation with Sid's driver's death. Sid's absence was explained as a burnout from work. It was communicated to Symbiotic Research Labs by the research director at Crypto Tech Pvt. Ltd, Sid's cover for an employer. It was explained that Sid had finally decided to take a vacation he had been planning for a long time.

The CIA's low level mercenaries in Pune were called off. They had easily given up their contact and Freddie was following the complex chain to its source.

In the meanwhile there was a surprising development. Professor Richard Levine had received a call from Sarah Johansson's boss at the lobbying firm where she worked. Richard had promptly got him in touch with Mitch Shelby. Todd Lester, Sarah's boss, had asked for immunity from prosecution. He had information he wanted to share with the authorities.

Mitch had initiated the legal process to evaluate the possibility. It was a brand new territory for him. He didn't quite care for it, but he was the director's point man on this evolving crisis. Mitch was determined to get to the bottom of who was the brain behind this sordid affair. The fact that his agent was drawn into this had made it Mitch Shelby's problem.

As far as the nuclear material was concerned, he had received assurances from the chief scientist at the Los Alamos lab. As long as the container was not opened either manually or by the crude timing contraption placed on it, it was perfectly safe to carry it. The low grade nuclear material could be handled easily once it was in Los Alamos. In fact the scientists were very curious to get their hands on what looked like a nuclear storage device from North Korea. Nobody had been able to actually analyze the spent nuclear material from North Korea. It would certainly augment their database and give them valuable information.

Mitch was worried more about the wider political implications. How did this North Korean nuclear material end up in Pakistan? There were strong suspicions that Iran was trafficking the North Korean nuclear material. Was Iran working with Pakistan? Was it part of the remaining tentacles of A.Q Khan's illegal nuclear bazaar? All these issues were way over the head of a digital security expert. What did he know about these issues? Mitch decided that someone else needed to step in to own various angles of this fast breaking affair. He would approach Director Osborne.

Communicating directly with a naval commander was far easier than Mitch had imagined. Once all the necessary clearances were obtained by the presidential order, he could use the CIA communication room to make direct contact with Vice Admiral Joel Newsome, in charge of the United States Navy's 5th fleet.

"Admiral Newsome, this is Mitch Shelby. I appreciate the help from your fleet sir." Mitch had not addressed an active duty naval vice admiral before.

"Mr. Shelby, you are most welcome. This is easy stuff. Are we picking your man and his cargo or just the cargo?" inquired the Vice Admiral.

"Just the container. It's about eighteen inches long and I would say about four inches in diameter. It must weigh a lot for its size as it contains spent nuclear material. I have been told it's perfectly safe to handle it as long as the container is not destroyed or opened."

Mitch was no nuclear expert. But he was merely repeating what he was told by the scientists. Mitch knew that fewer the number of people involved, better the chances were of keeping this affair under wraps as the director had demanded.

"I will let you know the precise coordinates as soon as I have them. I will instruct my agent to plan the handover at night when it's dark. I suppose it's not a problem." Mitch said.

"It's not a problem. And of course we can do it. In fact I would require that it be done at night. India is a friendly nation but they will go berserk if they find the U.S. navy encroaching their territorial waters." Vice Admiral Newsome quipped.

CHAPTER 47

Their rental car pulled off the hotel driveway on to the main road leading away from the airport. The driver was an elderly man who introduced himself as Mr. Mishra. Sid was used to having a driver and he gave the driver instructions in English. Mr. Mishra informed him that they will take the old Pune highway to start with and then take highway NH17 towards Goa.

Sid could not get over the image of Anand's body slumped over the steering wheel of his car. *Who had killed his driver? And why?* There were more questions than answers. *How was Brad Malone involved in this?* The fact that Mitch Shelby had specifically instructed Sid not to call Brad had surprised him. Brad was his main contact with the CIA thus far. Brad was the face of the CIA as far as Sid was concerned.

There were so many questions swirling in his head. Too many unresolved issues to give anyone a headache. But now he was with Sarah. It made him feel so good. Sarah had come all the way to India looking for him, thinking he was in trouble. That spoke volumes of her love for him. And Sid had reciprocated. He had set things straight with her, making his feelings for her known in no uncertain terms. Now that they were spoken for each other, it seemed as if it was always meant to be this way. *Why was there any doubt in his mind before?*

Their car navigated the Mumbai traffic and crossed a bridge to go over the body of water separating Mumbai from the mainland to the East. The route so far was familiar to Sid. On his many trips between Pune and Mumbai he had traversed this road before.

Sid was excited to finally visit *Konkan*, the land of his ancestors. Sarah was curious to know where they were going, but Sid couldn't help her too much as he didn't know a lot either.

Sarah of course knew of the impending transfer of the contents of Sid's backpack to U.S. servicemen. *It'll be good to get rid of this sinister thing,* Sarah had thought.

Her mind went back to the conversation she had with Todd Lester, her superior at Arnold & Gregg. It was a bizarre coincidence that Todd in some way was actually involved with what was going on with Sid. She had sensed that Todd was on the wrong side of the equation but perhaps not on his own volition. The good news was that he wanted to come clean, make amends. Before she left for India, Todd had talked to her one more time. Sarah had passed on Professor Levine's number, as that was the only contact she knew of. The sooner it all got taken care of, the better it would be for her and Sid. Now that she knew they had a future together, she was eager to get there.

An hour and a half had passed since they left the hotel. The scenery outside changed from the crowded streets of Mumbai. After a while they once again encountered crowded streets of an area called *Navi Mumbai* or New Bombay. Soon after that the surroundings transitioned to peaceful, rural setting. The road didn't have much traffic. There were an increasing number of rolling hills. The road was constantly turning, as if the car had to take a leisurely stroll through the sometime gentle and sometimes tight curves. The verdant landscape had a calming effect on both of them. The constant turns were pushing them against each other, as if to provide an excuse to be close to each other. They drove for several hours. Their driver stopped the car couple of times for tea break before reaching a town called *Khed*. This is where he explained they would leave the National Highway 17 and embark on smaller roads towards their destination, *Murud Beach*.

This time of the year, *Konkan* was a beautiful country side with its numerous streams and rivers filled with water, bringing dense greenery to every hill they touched, like a magic wand. Sarah was reminded of her favorite movie and the Shire of the Hobbits. This could have easily been the setting for the picturesque home of Tolkien's magical creatures. As they left the highway, traffic became a curious mixture of 21ˢᵗ century cars comingling with animal pulled carts and everything in between. Sarah was just mesmerized by the sights and sounds around her. She was glued to the car window like a small child riding a train for the first time. Even though the vehicle drivers made liberal use of their horns, nobody looked stressed. It was somehow an integral part of the routine, sometimes warning specific pedestrians to watch out and sometimes it was a loud complaint against a slow driver refusing to yield to faster vehicles. And the sound varied accordingly, from a quick polite beep to a sustained shrill noise.

From the town of *Khed*, they drove to a regional hub town of *Dapoli*. Sid had heard from his father of *Dapoli* and the many great sons of the soil who had made major contributions to the Indian nation. The drive from *Dapoli* to *Murud* was especially beautiful. It was a rustic, peaceful land where his ancestors had lived for many generations since their arrival to these shores in ships so long ago.

Sid was both excited and tense at the same time. He had not contacted Mitch Shelby in a long time. He was nearing the end of this unwanted adventure. An adventure he had not signed up for but found himself in the center of. He hoped Mitch would come through as promised. The thought of carrying that backpack for another day was unbearable.

It was early evening by the time they reached their destination at the *Murud Beach*.

The hotel, or the resort as its sign proclaimed, consisted of several modest free standing buildings, each a guest room. The rooms were clean, air conditioned and decorated attractively but in a simple way.

They checked in at the front office that was more of a free-standing kiosk. A beautifully landscaped dirt path led Sid and Sarah to the entrance of their room. A little distance away at the center of the resort was the dining area. It had a roof of cut and dried coconut leaves and was open from all sides except for unobtrusive walls of thin plastic mesh to keep insects away. And the beach was about fifty feet away from their room.

It was no Destin, Sid thought to himself, thinking of his family's favorite beach spot along the Gulf of Mexico in Florida's panhandle region. But it would do. A bellboy brought their bags to the room. Sid tipped him and got down to business.

He opened his laptop and powered it on. Mitch had asked him to be right on the spot where he could stay for at least half hour for the pickup. Although Sid didn't want the Navy SEALs to have to come into the resort, he wanted to give Mitch heads up of his current location. Sarah wanted to take a shower. As she stepped in the bathroom, Sid stepped outside with his laptop and walked briskly to the soft sand where he could see and hear the waves.

It was after sunset. The twilight was disappearing fast. Sid spotted a bench at the edge of the hotel property. He sat down and started the GPS application. The screen came up alive with the latitude and longitude of his location. Sid took out the prepaid phone his aunt had given him and powered it up.

Luckily he was getting decent reception and could place a call to Mitch. He read out his coordinates to Mitch and they agreed for the pickup to be within two hours to two and half hours from then.

As Sid was speaking to Mitch, Hafez and his assistant were lurking behind a thick brush at the northern edge of the hotel property where the landscaped compound met the sandy beach.

"*Chalo, sale ko uda dete hai*" his assistant said in hushed tone. He was suggesting they kill Sid then and there.

Hafez shushed him. He was getting annoyed by this local hit man. No training, no discipline, Hafez cursed under his breath. "*Pagal hai kya?* Keep that revolver out of sight, you fool."

He had to make sure of what Sid Joshi was up to. Hafez had received accurate information from his contact in Mumbai. He had the exact address where Sid and his female companion were headed. It was easy for Hafez to drive to *Konkan*, barely an hour behind Sid and Sarah. He had reached *Murud Beach* just as it was getting dark. He had driven non-stop except for a short tea break.

He had parked the car about two hundred meters away from the resort. The road that passed for the main thoroughfare in *Murud* was a dark narrow lane. There were no street lights and hardly anyone was out and about at this hour. It had suited Hafez and his assistant quite well. They had walked along the northern edge of the resort property. Security detail was non-existent. There were two watchmen employed by the resort. They would wield just sticks for a weapon. They usually kept stray dogs away from the resort and sometimes doubled as bus boys on a busy day.

Today was not a busy day. Except for the American couple, there was one family with young kids, and they had already retired to their room for the night after an early dinner.

Hafez could get a good view of the cottage where Sid and Sarah were staying. He decided to keep round the clock watch. He would take a nap on the beach while his assistant watched the cottage.

"Kuch pagalpan mat kar na. Kuch nazar aaya to muze batana" he said chidingly, instructing his assistant to not do anything foolish and to wake him up if anything was afoot.

CHAPTER 48

ZULU 0100:

Vice Admiral Joel Newsome had ordered a four men SEAL unit to be flown onto a frigate that had been dispatched to patrol the commercial shipping lanes off the coast of Somalia. The frigate had left Manama, Bahrain three days ago and was six hundred miles east of the coast of Oman. The mission of the SEAL team was clandestine. They would be deployed in a fast moving rubber watercraft in the international waters off of India's coast. The precise location was unknown at this time. Their mission was to recover a small object from a friendly party consisting of a male and a female agent on a beach at this yet to be determined location. They were to bring in the container safely, without shaking, or dropping it as it was an unarmed bomb. The exact nature of the bomb was classified information and was not shared with the SEALs.

After the SEAL team was dropped on its deck, the frigate was ordered to alter its course and head full speed towards India, to be positioned somewhere in the international waters about one hundred and sixty kilometers south of Mumbai. The frigate was small in footprint. It was not expected that the Indian navy would spot it. But just in case, the Vice Admiral had readied a communiqué to explain its presence for his counterpart in the Indian navy. Joel Newsome hoped it wouldn't come to that.

ZULU 1400:

Mitch hung up the phone. Once again he was relieved that Sid had not panicked and had managed to find his way to the West coast of India without being followed. He was certain that the CIA mercenaries were not following Sid anymore, but as corroborated by Freddie Solomon, he expected that the Pakistanis had deployed agents to recover what was theirs. Freddie was toiling assiduously to work his way up the chain of communications and funds transfer between the mercenaries and whoever employed them. Separately, Mitch was busy piecing together what he could with help from Todd Lester, his own man Brad Malone, and several of the Pentagon's covert mission experts. The President had ordered the Secretary of Defense to conduct a full internal investigation if any of the Pentagon's staff was complicit in this plot.

Mitch had Sid's coordinates and he passed them on to the Vice Admiral Newsome's staff. The rendezvous was scheduled within two hours.

The orders and the destination were conveyed to the SEAL mission team.

ZULU 1500:

Sarah finished her shower. She was dressed in jeans and a T-shirt. Sid had returned to their room after contacting Mitch Shelby. Sarah was sitting at the edge of their bed, putting on her shoes. Sid sat down next to her and held her hand. They both were tense in anticipation of the impending transfer. The transfer of the 'evil backpack' as Sarah had termed it. It was her attempt to bring some levity to an otherwise serious situation.

"It's time to go." Sid said. "You know you don't have to do this. I can go by myself. It's just a matter of handing over the backpack to the SEALs." Sid tried to frame it as a routine activity. But Sarah wouldn't budge.

"I am going with you. Perhaps we can go for a stroll afterwards if it's going to be that easy." She said. Sid realized there was no way to persuade her.

They left their room. They took steps down to the landscaped path. It was dark outside. The lighting in the resort area was quite poor, which suited them well. They wanted to be less visible. From their room, they walked towards the dining area. There were no other guests in the dining area at this time.

Earlier in his room, Sid had carefully removed the container, placing it on the floor. He had emptied his backpack of all other contents that he routinely carried to work every day. Then he placed the cylindrical container back in the backpack, strapping it down tight so it wouldn't shake. He also packed a flashlight he had purchased in Mumbai. As per Mitch's instruction, when Sid went shopping with his aunt in *Dadar*, he had purchased a powerful flashlight for signaling the reconnaissance team.

The dining room staff seated them at a table and brought cold bottled water and menus. Sid ordered for both himself and Sarah. He then kept his backpack next to Sarah and decided to take a quick walk around the dining area. There wasn't anybody around that he could see. A few of the staff were cleaning the open ground, picking up trash and tiding up chairs and benches. Sid felt better after walking around. It helped him somewhat to alleviate the tension building up in his body.

Just as Sid and Sarah were walking towards the dining area, Hafez was woken up by his assistant.

"*Woh log bahar aa gaye. Khana khane ja rahe hai.*" The assistant told Hafez that their subjects had emerged from the room and were going to the dining area.

Hafez jumped to his feet. He observed Sid and the girl reach the dining area. This guy Sid was carrying his backpack. That is unusual, thought Hafez. It was looking promising. After all the trouble he had been through, he may obtain what General Chaudhry so desperately wanted him to get. There will be a big payoff, Hafez was sure of that.

Hafez thought of boldly attacking the couple to confiscate the backpack. But there were several servers in the dining area. It would cause a commotion. And his orders were not to cause any killings if he could avoid it. It would be easy enough to break into the room at night and grab the backpack or any other belonging at gun point. What if the object he was looking for was not in the backpack, but in the room? Hafez decided to wait and watch.

The dinner tonight consisted of the local cuisine. Fish curry and rice was the staple food in these parts. The kitchen staff had also made bread called *naan* and butter chicken to suit their guests with low tolerance for spicy food. Sid's, or for that matter Sarah's, heart was not in dinner. They were both constantly casting furtive glances to their watch.

When they finally finished dinner, it was time to take a walk on the beach. For the benefit of any onlookers, they were holding each other's hand; a romantic couple taking a stroll on the beach.

ZULU 1600:

It was 9:30 p.m. local time. Sid and Sarah walked hand in hand onto the short walkway leading to the soft sand. Except for the low powered light at the end of the walkway, the beach was engulfed in complete darkness. The air was still warm but not uncomfortable, especially because of the soft westerly sea breeze.

Sid took out the flashlight from his backpack. It was one of the things Mitch had asked him to keep ready. His instructions were to use a flashlight to signal the navy SEALs. In spite of accurate coordinates, such human to human communication was of vital importance.

Hafez and his assistant crouched beyond the brush where they were hiding. They had to keep Sid in sight which was proving to be difficult as even the faint light of the resort lamppost faded away towards the water line. Hafez was getting curious. *What were they doing on the beach at night?* He pulled out his revolver and his assistant was only too happy to pull out his.

Sid and Sarah walked the short length of the boardwalk connecting the resort to the beach. They stepped into the sand. It was unusual that they were both still wearing tennis shoes. Sid wasn't sure what exactly awaited them. *What if they needed to run?* Having tennis shoes on would be helpful. They walked about hundred feet directly in front of the resort. It was a low tide. They stood in ankle deep water, their shoes and cuff of jeans soaking wet. The wait had begun. Sid had the flashlight ready in his left hand and he clutched the backpack strap in his right hand.

Hafez and the assistant moved out in the open. Hafez scanned the beach in both directions along the waterline. There wasn't anyone in sight. Dim lights of several fishing boats were visible almost a kilometer away in the sea.

ZULU 1620:

The inflatable watercraft was amazingly fast. It was equipped with a powerful and specialized engine that was whisperingly quiet. The four men SEAL team had launched from the frigate some twelve miles away, in the international waters. The frigate was in constant communication with the CENTCOM in Bahrain. There was no patrolling activity by the Indian navy in the vicinity of the frigate. There were several fishing boats scattered around. The fishing boats will be returning to the *Harnai-Murud* harbor which was about a mile north of where Sid and Sarah were, so the fishing boats were actually a good cover for the watercraft used by the SEALs. If someone was watching closely from the sky, it could be mistaken as just another fishing vessel.

The SEAL team reached within two hundred yards of the shore and stopped. Their plan was to traverse the remaining distance only after positive confirmation from the team on the ground.

One of the SEALs picked up a waterproof flashlight and pointed it towards the shore. Two quick flashes followed by a five second pause and two quick flashes again. He waited for fifteen seconds and repeated the sequence. As expected, this time the same exact sequence was reciprocated by someone on the shore and then followed it by three quick flashes.

Hafez noticed the flashlight signals. It suddenly dawned on him that something was afoot. What looked like a romantic stroll at night was actually a rendezvous.

But with whom? Hafez had not expected anyone to be coming from the sea. He must act quickly. The events unfolding were so unexpected that Hafez was paralyzed for a moment. He was afraid that his quarry may just disappear into the sea leaving him empty handed. *Unthinkable!*

Sid's return signal was the confirmation the SEAL team was waiting for. They sped towards the source of the flashlight raising the engine out of the water at the last minute to avoid damage to the propeller. Within seconds the watercraft was resting on sand bottom in about two feet of water. Two of the men in wet suit got out and ran towards the two figures standing in ankle deep water. As they approached, they kept their weapons ready in case the ground team they were to rendezvous with was compromised. This was the hardest part of their mission, not knowing what had unfolded on the ground in a foreign country. Getting caught was not an option.

As the two SEALs were moving forward, Hafez spotted them. He immediately grasped the fact that he was about to be outsmarted. He rushed forward, his weapon out in his extended hand. It was pointed directly to Sid's head, only twenty meters away as he moved parallel to the water line. His assistant had moved towards the back, away from the water. Between the two of them they had covered Sid's back and his right flank.

"Stop or I will kill them both." Hafez shouted loudly, addressing the SEAL who was now within twenty feet from Sid. The Navy SEAL stopped in his track. *Who was a friend and who was a foe really?*

The SEAL had his instructions drilled into him by practice. The safe and the hazard phrases were in place, as he was briefed. He called out loudly.

"Are you fucking around? Who is playing ball here?"

Playing ball was the phrase Sid was given by Mitch Shelby. Sid blurted out.

"I am if you care to know, but I am no Yankee fan."

The SEAL knew the score instantaneously. Sid had used the correct hazard phrase. The SEAL now knew that Sid was the agent and that he was in danger.

The second SEAL had covered the distance alarmingly quickly. In an instant both SEALs fell to the sand and fired their silenced weapons to injure Hafez. Hafez screamed with pain as he was hit in his right shoulder and in arm that was holding the gun. His gun dropped in the sand as he too fell down, his left hand clutching his right shoulder.

Hafez's assistant was dazed by the lightening fast and deadly fire coming from the SEALs. Before he could get his composure, a bullet struck his abdomen making him double over and fall. The SEALS intended to injure, not kill. The exchange had not taken place, and the mission was not accomplished yet. Any type of complication may arise and they knew that dead men don't answer questions.

In the meanwhile, the other two SEALs, quickly got out, picked up the watercraft and turned it around. They would get a running start pushing the watercraft in water as the two of their teammates returned. They were also vigilant, watching the action using night vision equipment. Since shots were fired, they both got out their Heckler & Koch HK416 rifles and were ready to intervene if needed. Under no circumstances would they leave their business unfinished.

Sid could hear his heart beating. Sarah was so tense she was forcefully clutching Sid's left arm. Sid was oblivious to the pain it was causing him. The two figures in wet suit approached them cautiously, now within ten feet. One of them shouted out.

"Are you fucking around? Who is playing ball here?" the same question again. The guns were now pointed towards Sid and Sarah.

Sid tried very hard not to make a mistake.

"That of course depends; if the White Sox win their division." He said carefully.

The two SEALs wanted to hear the words 'White Sox', which was the safe phrase.

They had positive confirmation that they were looking for. One of the men came forward as Sid handed him the backpack. *The backpack that had become part of his body for the past day and a half.* The SEAL took out a waterproof sack from his belt and put the backpack in it, sealing the sack quickly.

"What do you want to do with these two?" one of the SEALs asked pointing to Hafez and his assistant.

Before Sid could answer, the question was answered by Hafez himself. He had crawled forward in excruciating pain and had just gotten his left hand on the gun. He tried to raise his gun to shoot. Before he knew it, two bullets from the silenced weapon found their mark, killing Hafez instantly. His assistant was met with the same fate when he tried to raise his gun in vain.

Presence of an enemy and the ensuing gunfight was not expected. But the SEALs were trained to deal with the unexpected. It was obvious to them that the CIA agent was not a professionally trained combatant. His companion agent looked as if she would collapse any second.

The SEALs made their decision.

"We will dump the bodies at sea." said one of them.

Then each picked a dead body in the fireman carrying style and they raced back to their watercraft which was already being pushed towards the sea by the other two. The two men dumped their load in the watercraft and jumped in the now moving watercraft. The watercraft sped away, disappearing in the darkness.

The whole exchange had taken less than forty seconds.

As he saw the four SEALs vanish in the night, Sid suddenly felt utterly exhausted. His legs felt weak and buckled under his weight. With a great effort he managed to collapse to a kneeling position. The waves were gently splashing on his hands and knees. He couldn't believe his ordeal was over. He had completed what he had to do and now he could rest.

Sarah kneeled next to him, her arms around his shoulders. She was sobbing. They sat there for what seemed like eternity. Sarah was the first to snap out of their nightmarish freeze.

"It's over Sid. Come on let's go back to our room and get some sleep. You'll be a new person tomorrow."

Sid pulled her toward him and kissed her. It was one touch he knew would tell him what was real and what was an illusion.

"You have the power to make me a new person. I am never going to let you go." Sid said smiling. "Now let's go home."

EPILOGUE

As it happens, more often than we may think, crises come and go. People who are affected by it deal with them, nations hopefully learn from them, but a vast majority of people don't know the difference.

Life goes on.

KARACHI, PAKISTAN:

The recent largess by the Americans, Pentagon in particular, had dried up. There was an internal investigation launched by the Pentagon. General Chaudhry's close friend, who was the number two man in Pakistan's embassy in Washington D.C., was under tremendous pressure to cooperate.

General Chaudhry had suffered setback on many fronts. First, the ISI was not happy with his last minute reversal to not deliver radioactive content. It was not discussed with the top generals and a personal decision to reverse the course was deemed to be an act of insubordination. On top of it, he had attempted to regain the dirty nuclear bomb using his personal influence without bringing in the ISI machinery. And his agent had failed to regain the bomb, outsmarted by a civilian neophyte, which resulted in the Americans quietly getting their hands on the nuclear material. It would be a nightmare to explain it all to the American President or the Secretary of State.

As expected, the Americans ratcheted up pressure to denuclearize. Over the years America had secretly pushed Pakistan to give up the nuclear arsenal in return for generous civilian aid. Of course all this stayed away from the public eye and perhaps will stay that way until Wiki Leaks gets hold of it someday.

General Chaudhry had many competitors within the ISI. They mounted pressure, demanding that he resign. General Iqbal Chaudhry had no choice. He resigned his post and moved to London to live a quiet, retired life.

ITHACA, NEW YORK:

Professor Richard Levine wrapped up his lecture. The topic was digital security. It was a small part of the course curriculum, but he had poured his heart into it. The students were stunned to hear of the breadth and ferocity of attacks that were never spoken of but were quite prevalent.

A few students followed him, carrying on the conversation. They all reached the professor's office. As he opened the door to his office, they saw a person sitting in a visitor's chair, his back to the door. The man was obviously waiting to see Professor Levine.

As he heard the door open, Mitch Shelby got up and turned to face Richard.

"Hello Professor Levine. May I have a word with you?" was his rhetorical question.

Then he turned to the group of students, winked, and said, "I was here first."

The kids laughed and left.

"Hello Mitch." greeted the professor. "What a surprise. What brings you to Ithaca? I hope you didn't just happen to be in the neighborhood. I don't have any students to spare for your cause."

Now it was Richard Levine's turn to wink.

The joke of course referred to Mitch's previous meeting at Richard's house in Ithaca. That meeting had led to a chain of events that ultimately took his favorite student on an unwanted adventure in a faraway land.

"No, I didn't just drop by. This is an official visit. The Director has especially asked me to thank you in person."

The two friends chatted for a while. Mitch told of a rather substantial NSA grant to be announced for the Department of Computer Information. He was going to send a formal communication to the Dean's office the next day.

WASHINGTON D.C.:

A lot of things transpired in this city. But as is its wont, most of the information was not announced, but leaked.

There was a closed door hearing at the Pentagon. The Secretary of Defense was furious to find out what went on in the name of saving America. He vowed to rid the Pentagon of any rogue elements (as if the rogue elements would just stand up when a roll call is announced.)

Oliver Martin survived. Nobody could pin any specific crime on him. The Pakistani diplomat invoked his diplomatic immunity and declined to cooperate. Under intense pressure from the State Department he was transferred back to Islamabad in couple of months.

Brad Malone was implicated on a lesser charge of not following the CIA procedures as it was again impossible to prove that he was the conduit to usurp Sid Joshi's presence in Pune for planting a dirty nuclear bomb. He resigned, and joined a private company as a mercenary. He also landed a semi-permanent talk show guest spot at a sympathetic TV channel.

The lobbying firm of Arnold & Gregg was rumored to be involved in arranging some illegal activities overseas. There were noises against the enormous power lobbyists wield in this town. But in the end, nothing happened. In influential circles notes were made of the Teflon-like qualities of the firm. Its clout was proven and it helped attract many new clients as a result.

Todd Lester resigned from his job. He patched up things with his wife Jill. The two moved to Virginia Beach and became active in a local church. The congregation was grateful for their social work and generous contributions.

Mitch Shelby continued his stellar career with the CIA. He concluded that there was no conspiracy to plant programmable defects or backdoor traps in embedded chip design. He, however, foiled several attempts by some not-to-be-named governments to sabotage many different sensitive targets, from the NASDAQ electronic stock exchange, to the power grid, to the SWIFT financial network. As usual, the good deeds and successes of the CIA were unknown and therefore went unrecognized by the general public.

MOUNTAIN VIEW, CALIFORNIA

Roger Patel was not even investigated beyond some probing questions, as he didn't have any direct or indirect knowledge of planting the nuclear material in India. He had not done anything illegal that could be proven in a court of law. Todd Lester's sealed testimony had clearly exonerated Roger Patel. Although records related to this affair were subpoenaed by the government, the firm of Arnold & Gregg didn't have any records to implicate Roger.

However, in his way of thinking, Roger had to face a higher court. It was the court of his board of directors. Roger was stripped of his dual positions as the CEO and Chairman of the board. A unanimous decision was made to hire new talent from outside.

Personally, Roger turned his defeats of the past several years into a challenge. He still had substantial personal wealth and a strong desire to succeed. He realized he was a business entrepreneur, not an inventor or a visionary. His strengths were in growing a small fledgling business to a commercial success and not necessarily in running the business beyond the initial spurt of growth. He formed a venture capital firm to acquire small companies with promise and sell them when they reached their full potential.

MURUD BEACH, KONKAN, INDIA:

The couple stayed at the resort beyond their initial one night booking. It was a slow season and the resort management was happy to accommodate. Their driver, Mr. Mishra, was willing to extend the car rental period. Mr. Mitch Shelby had insisted that Sid take some time off. The CIA would make arrangements to fly them home first class whenever Sid was ready.

Sid had his wish come true. He got a chance to see the land of his ancestors up close. With Sarah, he crisscrossed the countryside. They took leisurely walks around fishing villages strewn across the coast. Culinary treats of fresh fish and shrimp from local catch were especially appetizing. Sarah tried in vain to ask for recipes. Sid's command on *Marathi*, the regional language, was passable at best, but he couldn't understand any of the cooking terminology nor was he familiar with names of spices or ingredients that were used.

The resort manager had become quite friendly with Sid. He insisted that they visit a local temple, tucked away in a picturesque setting on the bank of a large stream, somewhere between *Murud* and *Dapoli*. Sid decided to stop there on one of his excursion. It was a small dilapidated building. There was a list of last names posted on a simple board on one of the inside walls. He had to reach back many years in his childhood days when he was exposed to reading Hindi. With some effort he was able to read the board. To Sid's surprise, he noticed his own last name in that list; written in *Devnagari* script. As the local priest explained, apparently it was the original worshipping place of ten families, including his, dating back several generations. Sid took lots of pictures so he could share the experience with his parents.

Getting some quality time with Sarah on a leisurely trip to India had not even registered in his dreams before. Sid was so happy he actually got a chance to do it. It helped erase the nightmare he had lived through the past several days. Sarah in turn had shared her feelings for him. There was no turning back. They both had found each other.

In one town, Sid slipped away for half an hour, giving Sarah some excuse. He visited a jewelry shop to buy a ring. The next day after breakfast, he dropped on his knee and asked Sarah to marry him. The dining area staff was very amused; they had never seen a man propose in this manner.

Sarah said yes!

The official engagement was to be in Washington D.C. Both families would of course be there.

They would plan their future together on the long flight home.